CUPID

BRITTNEY LAUREN

Editing by Ellies Edits

Proofreading by Lily Alcala

Author's Note

Welcome to Cupid.

This is a spicy, open door romance intended for mature readers, eighteen and older. While the romance is the main focus of this story, there are a couple of elements that may be triggers for some people; including familial emotional abuse and body shaming. Every book isn't for everybody, and that's okay.

Also, if we're related, this may be a good time to put the book down or at least proceed with caution. Otherwise, I won't be able to look you in the eye.

xo, Brittney

For the overlooked and the under appreciated.
And for Carole who wanted to know when my books were going to get spicier.

Love looks not with the eyes, but with the mind,
And therefore is winged Cupid painted blind.
– William Shakespeare, A Midsummer Night's Dream

CHAPTER ONE

JANUARY 30

DESPERATION ALREADY DOES FUNNY things to a single, ovulating thirty-year-old woman. Add in the calendar reminding me Valentine's Day is only two weeks away, and desperation isn't a strong enough word. There is a prominent, rational part of my brain that knows February fourteenth is simply just another date; a date with no real meaning in what it's like to feel desired. But for the next two weeks, all things love and doily will blanket my town, and the irrational part of my brain will light up like a fluorescent vacancy sign, making the loneliness feel inescapable.

Cupid clearly has a vendetta against me. Instead of hitting me with his arrows, he flies over town only to flip me off while calling me a virgin loser. And while I'm not *technically* a virgin, the day is still hard. Although what else can you expect when you live in a town named after the tiny baby angel. Cupid, California—a remote Northern California town, light-years away from real society. Where people look at you like you're on death's doorstep if you're a woman who's not married with two kids by twenty-five. To them I'm basically a walking corpse.

This year though, everything is changing because I'm finally going to feel what it's like to be desired. And it was all by accident.

It was the one good thing that came out of another failed first date. I went from being stood up by a wisp of an apparition in the shape of a man to falling into an internet deep dive to see if sex clubs were real. How I got from one point to the other is a bit blurry though. All I know is I was champagne drunk on my couch when I stumbled upon Midnights; Silicon Valley's exclusive sex club.

Where your darkest desires meet the light.

Or at least that's what their website said.

All I want is to know what it feels like to be wanted, even if it's only for one night, even if it's only for my body. Someone who trips over themselves at the very thought of me. Someone who won't see my lack of experience as a way to mold me into what they want, but to help me figure out what I like. And I think Midnights can give me that.

Maybe it was too much to ask for from a sex club, but I'd rather grasp at the possibility than linger in dating app purgatory forever.

My only issue is that Midnights cost money. A lot of money, like hand over your entire paycheck, and maybe a week's admission is covered, type of money. Too much money if you really ask me and so far out of any budget I can justify with my small government employee salary, that's for sure.

Except every year Midnights hosts an open house, where potential members can come and see the club...as long as they accept your application. Even their open houses are exclusive, which, after reading through every scrap of information I found on Midnights, it's understandable. In a drunk induced haze, I filmed a quick introduction video, answered a few required questions and submitted my application.

There was a good chance they would take one look at my video submission and delete it without a second thought. Which is why I never breathed a word of this to anyone. A terrible breach of girl code 101, but if I have to listen to another one of my married friends placate me with an 'it'll happen, when it happens' speech, I'll die.

Actually die.

Weeks passed after that night and for a while I thought maybe I made it up. Perhaps I consumed way more champagne than I thought and it was all a dream. I told myself it was fine, that I didn't need Midnights. That my life may be mundane but it was mine.

Except two nights ago, what I thought was just a dream turned out to be very real when a pristine white box showed up in my mailbox. Inside was a oxblood colored envelope with an invitation that read *Anonymity in the Presence of Pleasure* along with today's date, an address, password, and a mask even my own parents wouldn't recognize me in.

My life is far from perfect, but at least I will have this one night. One night where I can forget about my family who'd rather me fade into oblivion and my crippling dread of how I think I might end up alone. One night where everything I've been craving will finally be within reach.

Living in Cupid means everyone knows everyone, and when your father is the mayor, it means they also know everything about my family. At least they think they do. Our entire family was perched on a pedestal because my father is in a position of power, but all the distance created is smoke and mirrors. No one sees how terrible they truly are. And there's no point in trying to get the town to notice, because that would ruin the illusion. The perfect family running the perfect town.

It's been this way my entire life; nothing ever changes and I don't think it ever will. My saving grace comes in the form of being the middle child and I'm often overlooked. No one asks about me, no one cares that I moved away for college or why I moved back to Cupid after so many years away, which is fine by me. I'll leave the spotlight for my siblings; they always look better in it, anyway.

Sometimes I wonder if it's exhausting for them. Living in our parents' shadows and under the scrutinizing eye of our town. Moving away was the best thing I ever did, and my parents were all too thrilled to send me off to Los Angeles for college instead of staying in town and settling down. I moved away thinking they were all in my rearview mirror, only coming home for the holidays and even that was only for the first couple of years. By the time I graduated and landed my first job as an art curator, I was down to only calling home for Christmas or birthdays, and I fucking loved it. The freedom was intoxicating.

Moving back to Cupid was the last thing I ever wanted, but there wasn't much to do when budget cuts took my position, and not only from my museum but from everywhere in my field. I spent months looking for a new job, delaying the inevitable until moving back was the only option. My parents were...less than pleased.

Still, my father couldn't let anyone know his daughter was a failure, so I came home with my tail between my legs, bags in tow and a job at City Hall in the recreation department waiting for me. It's dull and not at all what I thought I'd be doing with my degree in art history. Most of my time is spent designing the activities magazine for the town every quarter, and revamping social media posts that no one ever interacts with.

Everything in Cupid is slow; the lives, the traffic, the baristas at the coffee shop. I feel like I'm moving at warp speed around a town that lives in slow motion. My creativity may be slowly withering away, but at least the months leading up to the Cupid's Ball gives me a creative outlet.

With two weeks until Valentine's Day, and a million tasks for the Ball piling on my already skyscraper tall plate, all I can think about is if my dress for tonight is too ridiculous and if it goes with the mask I received. All while trying to convince myself not to chicken out.

I stop scrolling through the department store website and toss my phone onto my desk. It's too late to change my outfit, but with any luck, I won't be wearing it for long anyway. My office door opens right as I give my mouse a little wiggle and I'm greeted with the pair of eyes that have a permanent time slot in my fantasies.

Glacier irises sweep across my office until they land on me, pinning me to my chair and making it hard to breathe. "Harper, do you have the briefings for your father's five o'clock?" His velvet voice demands as he stalks closer to me.

You can list every panty-dropping quality a man can possess, and Nolan Archer surpasses each one without even trying. Impossibly tall, so even on the days I wear my highest heels, my face is still only level with his chest. Full, wavy chocolate brown hair with streaks of silver through the sides, and a smile that melts me into submission whenever there's a hint of it on his plush lips.

He is perfect in almost every single way.

"Harper," he snaps. "Your father's waiting."

In every way except that he's my boss who's also kind of a dick.

"Yes, Sir," I feign with a mock two finger salute and a heavy eye roll.

Nolan's jaw clenches, bright eyes flaring to life. "The file," he says. Voice straining and swallowing back unspoken words.

It takes me a second longer than normal but I tear my eyes from his unusual display of restraint and search my mess of a desk for what he requested. "Yes, it's riiiight—" I drag out the word until my fingers curl around the bindings of the reports I put together last night before heading home. "Here!" I exclaim, holding them up like a trophy.

With four long strides, he moves swiftly and plucks them from my grasp. No "thank you", no "I'm so glad you had time to do this last night even though I told you five minutes before you normally go home."

Nothing. Nada. Zilch.

Instead, he quickly thumbs through the pages. Lips mashing together in a hard line like he expects to find a mistake.

He won't, but he still looks.

"We should only be there for an hour. Can you make sure next week's budget is in my inbox by the time we're done?"

"You know I'm not your assistant, right?"

He looks up from the reports, and my next breath disappears. I really wish there's something I can do about this...is it still a crush when you're this old? Nolan has a hold on me and us working in the same building every day is only making it worse.

"What?"

"I'm not your assistant, you're my boss, but only because I'm a one woman department. That's what Sadie's for, and she should have sent you the budget two weeks ago. If you don't have it, take it up with her."

He drags his tongue along his top teeth while continuing to stare at me. A few seconds in I forfeit and glance over at my computer screen. The file in question is staring at me from my desktop because Sadie, while also another breathtaking human somehow stuck in government work, is kind of useless and I figured she would have forgotten to forward it along after I sent it to her to put the meeting on his calendar.

"Harper," Nolan says in a low, rocky tone. The deep baritone sound shoots straight to my core, flushing every inch of my body in a heat I'm afraid he'll see if he looks closely. And the last thing I need is for Nolan to find out the types of thoughts I'm harboring about him.

"Fine," I click open an email and attach the file I was always going to send him. "But for the love of God, once you're done with this secretary, can you please get one with a brain?"

Without an answer he turns and leaves, finally allowing me a chance at a full breath. Except it's tainted with the smell of him. Rich notes of smoky woods, trapping me in a forest that's hard to find my way out of. For months I've tried to figure out what he wears, spending an ungodly amount of time in the fragrance department and have never been able to pinpoint it.

Knowing him, it's probably some imported scent where one bottle alone costs more than I make in a month. It would be impossible for me to figure out but then most things concerning him are, like why he's even in Cupid.

Six months ago Nolan left his job as CEO of his family company, only to show up and take over as City Manager. For weeks the town talked only of him, and normally I might have leaned into the gossip except we've known each other for years, or at least we've known *of* each other.

My father is a born and bred Cupid man, and as is Nolan. The two were best friends all throughout school until high school graduation, when Nolan went to one Ivy League school and my father another. My father came back to Cupid, Nolan avoided it like it was on fire. They kept it touch, but the years whittled them down to Christmas card acquaintances until he showed up in town and is suddenly City Manager. I'm not too sure running a conglomerate company translates well to running a small valley town, even if it was founded by the same family two hundred years ago, but who am I to say?

I never thought twice about Nolan over the years, he's my dad's friend, why would I? But suddenly I'm sharing the town with him and my mind is reduced to one track. Whenever Nolan is around, my brain turns off, my libido flips on and skyrockets off the charts. It's a real problem.

I need to spend the next two weeks in party planning overdrive and not thinking about Nolan. Which is easier said than done. At least I'll have my one night at Midnights to get me through it.

CHAPTER TWO

Nolan

"SADIE," I BARK, WALKING into the small foyer before my office. A long way from the high-rise corner office I once occupied in the Bay Area, but who's keeping track? Sadie practically jumps out of her seat at the sound of my voice, her platinum blond hair bouncing with movement and the nail file she's holding goes skidding across her desk.

Zero attempts to hide she was fixing her nails when she should have been working.

What's new though? I'm convinced Sadie thinks of herself as more ornamental than a government employee. Why she works here is beyond me.

One delicate hand presses against her chest as she blinks up at me with dull, stagnant water-blue eyes. Sadie takes a few seconds to straighten up, running her hands down the front of the obscenely tight dress and brushing back the loose curls around her face before looking back at me, her gaze switching and toeing the line of predatory. Every movement is for my benefit and I try not to think of the way it makes my stomach sour.

"Yes, Mr. Archer?"

Whatever she's doing to her voice only solidifies my bad mood. It's too high pitched and too soft all at once, and I know it's fake, her voice isn't even remotely that annoying when she's on the phone or talking to literally anyone else in the building.

Maybe this whole show she puts on for me is done absentmindedly? Maybe I'm reading too far into it? Maybe I'm the problem?

But then her hands skate back up her stomach and I have to take back the thoughts immediately. The display is extremely deliberate. What I want to know is what the hell was Dan thinking when he hired her?

"You never sent February's budget over," I say, doing my best to remove any sort of emotion from my voice.

Confusion creeps across her face in real time "The budget..." she says slowly, eyebrows pulling together.

"You know what, never mind, I asked Harper to send it over already."

Sadie's face pinches at the sound of her name, and I hate that as much as I loathe her voice. "Sorry, Mr. Archer," she calls out as I turn my back without bothering to respond, leaving to walk the length of City Hall to the Mayor's office for our meeting.

Dan Hawthorne sits in an overly large leather chair, with reading glasses perched on the end of his nose staring at his computer as I barge in.

"Eyes messing with you old man?" I joke, slipping into the seat across from him.

"Just you wait, you're only a year younger than me. One morning you'll wake up and realize you can't see a damn thing unless you hold it a foot from your face." He pulls the glasses off his face and tosses them onto the desk. "Do you have the report?" he asks, holding out one hand and scrubbing the other down his face.

I drop the packet in his waiting palm and then flip mine open to the first page. Dan mimics my movement, and without missing a beat, we dive into the new policies being implemented in Cupid come February first. A standard meeting of a long list of never ending appointments.

One look at my work calendar would send most people into a spiral until they quit on the spot. Somedays that exact thought crosses my mind too, but it's nothing compared to the responsibility of being CEO at Archer Enterprises, so I make do. And it was either City Manager in Cupid, or running one of the non-profits in the Midwest, and I can't bring myself to fall that low quite yet.

Like clockwork, we're done within the hour. "The report was well done, did Sadie put it together?" Dan asks out of nowhere, setting off an internal bell. Since I've been back, he's brought up Sadie more than anyone else at City Hall. I've gone through three secretaries, and not once did Dan ever bring them up in conversation. I'm not sure he even knew their names.

A disapproving grunt came from my chest. "No, it wasn't Sadie. Also where did you even find that girl? All her lights are on, but no one's home."

Dan barks out a laugh, shaking his head as he gathers up his briefcase and computer bag. "She's the daughter of one of Sherry's friends from the club. Her father is big in real estate development."

"Real estate?"

He hums in response.

One thing about Dan is nothing is done by accident. He's brilliant, but lazy, which is why he never left Cupid. Cupid is as small as it gets, leaving Dan the biggest fish. A big fish that's been talking a whole lot about plans for the outskirts of town since I showed up.

"I also knew she ticked off a couple of your boxes so I thought it would've been a good match." A downfall of the mayor being one of my longest friends is he thinks he knows me.

"Well you thought wrong, and you have no idea what I even go for. So please for the love of God, don't try and set me up again."

He stands from his desk, powering off his computer. "Oh, I know your type. Young, hot, tits big enough to drown in, does that sound about right?"

Okay, maybe he does know, but it feels strange coming out of his mouth when there's a particular woman in this building who fits that description and it sure as fuck isn't Sadie.

I shift uncomfortably on my feet before following him out of his office.

"Come on, man, you've been single for how many years? Why not give her a chance?" he says before lowering his voice "It's got to be better than paying for it."

"I don't pay for sex, dick."

He halts me with a look. "You don't belong to Midnights?"

I don't answer.

"Exactly. You're sitting on a fucking fortune, I'll never understand why you pay to belong to a club when you can get any woman you want."

I'm not about to stand around and spell out all my kinks for him, but I have reasons. For one, I pay a membership fee because once I'm inside those doors, my fortune has nothing to do with why women are with me. Most of the time, at least.

"Have a good night, Archer. And don't work too hard, it's not like you'll get a raise and we both know you don't need it."

"I won't," I call after him and watch as he walks out of the glass front doors as a desolate winter sky blocks any sliver of sun. January is cruel but what's worse is being heir to an almost billion dollar company, losing your position, only to be exiled somewhere you never wanted to come back to so you can't cause problems.

Cupid's small, so small that someone with my...proclivities would have a hell of time finding the right outlet. Women here only seem to want the same thing—a husband, two-point-five kids, and a golden retriever. Then I showed up, and all the unwed women ages nineteen to twenty-four seem to be everywhere I go with dollar signs in their eyes when they look at me.

Luckily, Midnights is situated between my last penthouse residence in the Bay Area and my much less conspicuous house on the outskirts of Cupid, so continuing my membership was an easy decision. It's far enough away and the monthly fee is more than the median household income here, so it's doubtful I'd run into anyone I know at the club.

Even if my schedule only opened up to where I go every few weeks it's still better than nothing. I have an outlet, and none of the women expect me to call afterwards.

My phone chimes and as I reach for it in my pocket I turn and head back to my office. The mayor might be able to leave at the same decent time every day but that's a life I know nothing about.

As if she has a direct line to my thoughts, Maxine's name pops up with a message.

> tomorrow night's open house, be there at 9

No 'do you have plans', no 'hi' or 'how have you been?' but I wouldn't expect anything else from Maxine.

> What if I said I have plans? Then what?

> don't be a brat

> Ahhh, but brats are your favorite.

I can practically hear the sigh heave from her chest through the phone. Maxine and I have been friends since college, and if there comes a time one of us isn't poking fun at the other, it's probably because one of us is dead.

> You haven't been here since before Christmas which was also the last time I saw you in general

> I've been busy. For being such a small town, Cupid somehow takes up all my time.

Tomorrow night, be here at 9. I'm trying out a new anonymous event for the open house. Your mask was delivered to your house this after-noon and there's no reason for you to really say no

If you missed me you could have just said so.

9 o'clock, Nolan

Fine, see you then.

I slip my phone back into my pocket and look up as the sound of heels clicking against the tile floor catch my attention. Dark hair ripples along Harper's back as she walks down the hall in front of me. Every step she takes pulls me further and further into a hypnotic sort of trance. One that is impossible to escape, not that I want to.

There are lists longer than I'll ever be able to read that spell out what constitutes a terrible person. There's the standard stuff—murder, people who steal candy from kids, grown men in crocs at the beach, the usual, and I'm about ninety-percent sure the images flowing through my head of my friend's daughter are on that list as well.

Harper stops at the water fountain, and like the greedy bastard I am, I stop moving so I can let my mind wander while I watch her. She bends at the waist and someone hits the slow motion button on my life. Water flows from the spout as she dips her head until it splashes against her pouty red painted lips. One of her hands holds all of her hair to the side to avoid it falling into the basin and I can't help but fantasize what it would be like to wrap it around my fist.

Can I wrap it around once or twice? If I thrust into her, what kind of noises will she make? Tiny whimpers of pleasure, or loud gasps that echo across the room?

If I told her how many times I've stopped to watch the way her tight skirts stretch over her round ass as she bends over and how it makes my hand itch to strike the soft flesh I know is underneath, would she blush, or cry out for more? Or both?

I hope if I ever find out, it's both.

God, I would do unfathomable things to get Harper Hawthorne bare and writhing underneath me. But instead I watch her from afar because there are a million boxes on why I shouldn't want her and every single one of them is checked.

Harper wipes away the drops of water that fell onto her chin with slow precision as she stands, too quick for me to react. She turns and locks eyes with me because I'm too focused on her to remember that I shouldn't be staring.

Even from this distance, I can see her brows scrunch together, and her dark eyes dart around to figure out why I'm hanging around in the middle of the hallway. I feel like a schoolboy, unable to control my desires when I'm near her. So I do the only thing I can think of, I turn on my heel without a word and walk in the opposite direction.

Maybe Maxine is right, I'll never tell her that, but it's been too long and maybe I did need to go to Midnights.

CHAPTER THREE

JANUARY 31

Nothing about the two hour drive to Midnights is sexy. I should have splurged for a hotel room and avoided this nervous sweaty trip all together.

Before leaving, I checked my reflection no less than a dozen times, and each time I found something new to agonize over. Either my dress was too tight, showing off too much of my stomach outline, or the slit was too high, leaving me thinking people would see the way my thighs rubbed together every time I took a step. Mascara keeps smudging under my eyes, slowly turning me into a raccoon and not giving the chic runway model I was going for. Nothing felt right, and trying to fix what's bothering me is an impossible task when everything and nothing is wrong at the same time.

Up until the second I walked out the door, I fought to tear the faux red silk from my body, plant my ass on my couch in my favorite sweats, and pretend I never found out about Midnights all together.

Who needs to come at someone else's hands anyway?

Apparently I do.

If I don't go tonight, I'll never get the chance again. Mainly because they only do the invitation only nights a few times a year and my name is sure to be blacklisted if I no-show my first time being invited.

One day when I'm old and grey, maybe even married for thirty years, I can look back and reminisce about the time I went to Silicon Valley's premier sex club.

But I can't do that if I don't get out of this car.

"Okay, you can do this, Harper. You want to do this," I say intently to my reflection in the rearview mirror.

"You're going to get out of this car, walk inside like you belong, and you're not leaving until you get what you came for." There's a woman looking back at me in the mirror, one I want to believe in but it still takes me a few more moments before I actually open the door and step out into the frigid January night. For a moment the inferno blazing under my skin tempers, allowing me a brief moment of reprieve. My dress is still too tight but I'm here and that's what matters.

Surprisingly, Midnights isn't in a popular part of the city; it's tucked away in an industrial neighborhood and if you didn't know to look for it, it's all too easy to miss. At first glance, it's weathered exposed brick with tall, wide windows in the front swathed in black fabric concealing everything that goes on inside. Not even music is making its way past the interior.

One thing catches my eye though, telling me this isn't some random building and it's a singular man standing outside the front door, dressed head to toe in black, blending in with the night. He clocks my slow approach toward the door from across the street and my fingers tighten on the mask clutched in my hands. It seemed silly to wear it walking up but the longer he stares, the more my self consciousness wraps around my stomach, trying to pull me back to my car.

No one else is walking up, so I use that to my advantage and scurry up to the door without anyone noticing my skyrocketing level of awkwardness.

"Hi," I squeak out. Tilting back my head, looking up at an emotionless face.

"Name," his gruff voice demands.

"Harper Hawthorne." When he makes no move showing he recognizes me, or at the very least my name, I relax a little. He presses his hand to the headset and mutters something to whoever is in the other line.

For a moment, I wonder if I'm about to be turned away.

Maybe they re-watched my video, felt the desperation rolling off of me, and decided they didn't need me dirtying up their, what I'm sure are, thousand count Egyptian cotton sheets.

Why else would it be taking so long?

I count a handful of heartbeats before he stops talking, and says to me, "You'll need to turn your phone off, and then you can head straight up the stairs, first door on your right."

He watches me like a hawk as I power down my phone and once he's satisfied steps to the side and is already looking back out to the street. A small tremble runs through my knees as I glide by him, through the doors and into the building.

Every inch of what I can see drips luxury as I step into the foyer and my jaw slackens as I take in everything all at once. With only a few feet between me and the staircase, I have little time to get a full view before I ascend them.

Hopefully this will be a quick meeting, giving me a little bit of time to peek around. There's also a very real chance no one will take interest in me and I stay in the main area the whole night. A shiver skates up my spine at the thought, my ego might not survive if that happens.

Jesus, even the railing feels expensive as I trail my fingertips along the mahogany grain, slowly making my way upstairs. Nothing about the experience is going to be ordinary, I knew that, but what I didn't expect was the sheer attention to detail. The membership fee is definitely being put to use.

Thousands of crystals strung together create the dazzling chandelier hanging over the first floor. Rich golden frames hang along the wall as I take each step up. Whoever designed this space deserves some sort of award because even little old me feels expensive simply by being here.

A nondescript door stands in front of me when I reach the second floor. Through the wood floats a feminine voice telling me to come in after my first knock. As I walk into the office, a stunning woman rises from behind an opulent wooden desk. "Harper, I'm Maxine. Welcome to

Midnights." Her voice is sultry and smooth as silk as she gestures to the seat in front of her. This is who my mind conjures up when I think sex clubs. This woman is sex wrapped in a tight, latex dress. She's elegant, strikingly beautiful, but most of all confident.

Maxine moves like every second of her time is valuable. Commanding attention, whether she's sitting down in her chair or flipping her long, glossy black hair behind her shoulder. Tiny acts I wouldn't even notice on someone else but with Maxine, I'm fixated. Immediately I decide, if I have the choice, despite the fact I'm already an adult, I want to be her when I grow up.

Her ruby red lips split into a sweet smile as she sits down, hands smoothing across the mahogany desk. "I have to say your video was my favorite out of all the applicants we saw."

A blush burns across my cheeks. "You saw that?" I ask, shrinking into myself.

Maxine chuckles. "Oh, yes, Midnights is my baby, nothing happens here that I don't know about and no one comes through those doors that I don't personally vet. It's what helps this place be so successful, a woman's touch does wonders."

My shoulders are practically in my ears. "Thank you?" I don't mean for it to be a question, but it tumbles out that way.

Making that video was one of the most vulnerable things I have ever done, and obviously someone was going to see it but I hoped to submit it and never think about it again. Let alone be face-to-face with the person who watched it.

Maxine's cat-like eyes snap to mine. "Please don't be embarrassed, what you said is exactly why I do these types of events. I know Midnights has this sort of..." One of her hands waves in front of her face, her golden watch glinting in the low light as she searches for what she wants to say. "Misconception attached to it. People who happen to stumble upon us without doing any research go right to sex and cheapen what actually happens here."

There's something satisfying about listening to someone speak about what they are passionate about, you can see the flames in Maxine's eyes as she continues.

She pulls a stack of papers from a drawer to her side, thicker than the budget proposals I put together at work for the Cupid Ball, and sets them in front of me. Then pulls a pen from a cup and lays it on the stack before continuing. "They're not wrong, obviously sex is happening here but they're not right either. Midnights is a place to explore who we are or who we want to be. I very much believe the best way to find ourselves is through our sexuality."

Yup, I definitely want to be her. I'm not sure if I've ever been so certain about anything in my life.

"I also really enjoyed that you were in sweats. Most people dress up or wear revealing clothing in their videos. There's nothing wrong with it of course, you were just refreshing to see. Reminded me of myself a little bit."

My eyebrows hit my hairline. Nothing is even remotely similar between us. Maxine is everything I want to be, and I'm well, I'm just me. Despite the years that might separate us, because honestly I can't tell if she's five or fifteen years older than me, I can't imagine that she's ever felt the way I do right now.

Her laugh gently ripples through the air as if she's reading my mind. "Before all of this, I too was a young woman trying to find my place in the world. You'll do great here, Harper, men and women will fall to your feet to teach you anything you want to know."

I swallow the lump of insecurity in my throat and nod.

We go over the endless amount of paper she pushes in my direction—NDA's, club agreements, a laundry list of rules, medical waivers—until finally she places a two page form in front of me.

"This is always my favorite part. Once you're done signing everything, this is the list you will go through to check off everything your heart desires. Things you want to try, positions you like, kinks you're into or may want more information about and such. If you match with someone, you'll receive a copy of each other's list to review, like an ice breaker of sorts. You don't have to review it, you can just talk, but I've found with newcomers it tends to be a bit easier this way."

My dress is back to being uncomfortably tight and with every passing second, all of this becomes more and more real.

She must notice, or maybe I'm overly obvious because her face softens. "Can I ask what you're looking for tonight?" Maxine asks after a moment of me simply staring at the mountain of paperwork in front of me.

What did I want from tonight?

Opening my mouth does nothing. Everything I want to say sticks like tar in my throat.

Leaning across the desk, Maxine pushes the paper out of my view. "There's no wrong answer."

No wrong answer. I almost want to laugh. What I want is so superficial even breathing a word about it makes my skin crawl, even though it shouldn't. I don't know why society tries to shove the notion that we shouldn't want to feel wanted, desired, or even sexual, but they did a damn good job of it in Cupid. No, we're much better off stuffing those feelings down and going about our lives like one of humans' basic needs doesn't even exist.

"I want to feel wanted," I answer with bitter tasting honesty. "It seems shallow to say out loud but I want someone to look at me and desire me. Someone who craves my pleasure as much as they do their own. But I'm so inexperienced that I also want someone to show me what I like." My next breath is heavy and sits uncomfortably in my lungs. "I'm always the person who is overlooked, in my family, in my job, with men. It doesn't matter where I am, no one sees me, and it's because of the way I look. Almost as if I'm undeserving somehow. I'm proud of this body, I love this body, but I also want to feel desired in this body."

My confession spills out of me, leaving behind a sour taste. The words are probably the most honest I've ever been and even with the taste coating my tongue, I can't help but feel more at ease.

"Harper, the things you want do not make you shallow, they make you human. It is basic biology to want those things. As women, we are often taught that our sexuality is shameful, that it's something we should hide or force out of ourselves, all the while men can stick their dick in however many people they want and no one bats an eye.

It's a cruel double standard that only exists to keep us reliant on them for our needs. But here at Midnights, you can be whoever you want, however you want, with as many people as you want, and no one here will make you feel as if it's wrong." That fire I saw earlier flares in her jewel tone eyes.

I can only manage a nod because anything else seems too grievous, and I really don't want to cry in front of her.

It's almost hard to even look at her, instead I let my eyes roam her office. Dozens of books line her shelves, some with names that make me blush and some more clinical than I would have expected. Her desk is bare, with only the papers I need to sign and a computer. No photos or anything to give away who she is outside of these walls but there's a chance there isn't even a difference. Finally my eyes snag on a large painting on the far wall.

It's beautiful. A winged man in the center; ethereal, and glowing amongst a chaotic background of what looks like demons. An image that feels like a dream and yet almost familiar.

"Eros, the Greek god of love, lust, and desire, or Cupid if you keep up with Roman mythology," Maxine says, interrupting my thoughts.

That's probably why it looked vaguely familiar. "I'm from a town called Cupid actually, so I am very aware of who he is."

For some reason my comment has Maxine tilting her head, a scheming sort of smile creeps across her lips. "Tonight, along with the masks, everyone will also have a code name, adding a bit more to the anonymity to the night."

"Oh, okay." Hopefully she doesn't expect me to have one ready to use because I don't even have a nickname.

"How do you feel about Psyche?"

I shrug. "Sure." That also seems familiar but my brain is overloading with information as I quickly look over the list.

"Midnights is a place to explore, and I hope you get that tonight. So take a look at the list, no need to rush, you have the entire night ahead of you, and when you're ready, put on your mask and join us downstairs," she says with an almost too chipper voice.

Words jump off the page as I scan the checklist. Some I knew, others I'm not even sure were real words. It's almost overwhelming. "What's Somnophilia?" I ask out loud, unable to contain my curiosity.

Maxine gets up from her desk as she answers. "A personal favorite of mine. I don't mean to run but I have a few more people to see before the fun starts. When you are done, you can leave it on the desk and come downstairs." She opens the door but before she leaves, she turns back to me, mischief glittering in her eyes. "I'm happy you're here, Harper, tonight may very well be the beginning of a new life for you," she says, and then disappears.

I think she might be right.

Chapter Four

Harper

Someone is going to take one look at this list and change their mind the moment they realize how boring I am. But there's no way half of these are real. I've gone through the paper three times and all I feel is plain. Only a handful are marked as a definitive yes, but are all so tame compared to everything else on the list.

A slough of boxes are marked as tentative but only because I knew the basis of what they are. Worse case if I end up with a partner who may be into one of them, I can probably ask what it really entails. Everything else is way over my head and might as well have been in Latin, and I'm too scared to put 'maybe' next to a word I don't know only to find out it's something I'm definitely not into.

Like 'water sports'.

Something tells me it has nothing to do with jet skis or even water. And since I was instructed to turn off my phone before I walked inside, I have no way to double check.

It takes me an entire hour to get through the list and another fifteen minutes to hype myself up enough to leave the office, but eventually I peel myself up off the chair.

The theater face mask is heavier than I expected. Not real gold, obviously, but still, the cool metal is a welcome sensation against my flush face as I slide it in place. It's a beautiful piece of art in and of itself, with the faux patina enhancing swirling details along the forehead and cheeks. I secure the ties around the back of my head and surprisingly a surge of confidence rushes through me once it's in place.

Not a single part of my face shows, nothing besides my eyes, and even then you can only tell the color. There are literally millions of people with brown eyes, I can be anyone. The whole point of tonight is anonymity, and I'm getting just that.

Tonight, I'm not Harper Hawthorne.

Tonight, I'm Psyche.

Tonight, I'm getting exactly what I want.

Pulling open the door, I'm hit with a shift in the atmosphere immediately. Softer light now fills the area, not so dim that you can't see much but enough to make everything feel intimate. Chatter floats up from below, meeting me half way up the stairs and my heart speeds up as my hands slide along the railing. By the time I reach the last step, I'm not sure if I'm excited or about to have a heart attack. If someone does speak to me right away, there's a good chance the first words out of my mouth are going to be something idiotic.

With a breath firmly stuck in my chest, I force myself to step into the main room. A few heads turn my way, lingering for a moment, their eyes cascading up and down my body, following me as I move further into the room. And another wave of confidence hit me like a lightning strike.

People mingle in small clusters in the open space, all in some form of mask that resembles mine. Mostly golds, a few decked out with pearls or glittering stones. Some of the more masculine masks have thick chains or are so dark it's like a black hole sits where their face should be. Those turn my stomach a bit and I scurry away as fast as possible when they turn my way.

It isn't packed like a club would be, instead it feels like I'd walked into an intimate party at a friend's house. Maxine is in the middle of the room, sans mask, talking to another statuesque woman and an even taller male. Her eyes quickly pass over me before giving me a slow approving smile and a tilt of her champagne glass.

I'm so far out of my league here, it's almost laughable but also feels right. Like I'm meant to be here, in this moment. It doesn't matter that men in suits, costing more than I can ever even dream of spending, surround me. Or that the room is filled with the kind of women you show pictures to surgeons and hang on your mirror as inspiration. Here, we were all on the same playing field.

But a little more courage can't hurt, and sometimes it's easiest to find at the bottom of a glass. A small bar sits in the far corner of the room and I quickly make my way over. When my hands hit the marble top, I'm taken back again; even if by some miracle I became a member here, I don't think I would ever get used to the grandeur of it all.

The bartender swiftly moves to my end once I catch his eye. "Hi, may I please have a glass of champagne?" My voice is a bit too squeaky, but he barely seems to notice as he grabs a crystal glass and sets it in front of me. Being drunk is the last thing on my mind, but I need something to curve the nerves clawing up from my stomach. A loud pop jolts my system as he pulls the cork from the bottle and a millions tiny bubbles fill the glass before he slides it toward me without a word.

Tipping my head back, the liquid hits my tongue and a weight falls off my shoulders, finally allowing me to breathe.

I don't quite know what to do yet. Mingle, obviously, but my feet feel rooted to the ground and it amazes me how I can want to be here and want to flee all at the same time. Downing half my glass in one gulp, I bargain with myself. I'm giving myself until the end of my drink to wallow in my awkwardness, and then I'll talk to someone.

But before I can take my next sip, a heavy presence washes over me. Fine hairs on the back of my neck stand at attention as goosebumps ripple across my shoulders and down my arms. Out of nowhere, a tiny voice in the back of my head, like a long forgotten sixth sense, whispers that someone is watching me.

With about as much stealth as a clumsy dog at dinner-time, I search for the perpetrator. My eyes roam over the groups, scanning for any sign of who set off my internal alarm, but no one is even looking my way. Disappointment flushes my chest. Something I thought I would never feel when thinking about someone lurking in the dark and staring at me.

One more sweep of the area, just in case, and something inside screeches at me to stop.

I swallow as I lock eyes with a man across the room.

Everything about him blends in with the dark corner he's standing in. Black slacks, black Oxford with the top two buttons undone, and luckily not one of those black hole masks that set off my flight response. Instead all I'm looking at is a simple full face mask, almost a carbon copy of the one I'm wearing but with masculine features, but it doesn't matter—every one of my senses flares to life as he stares.

A fire ignites where I stand, flames licking up my body the longer it goes on. Where goosebumps pricked only seconds ago, a steady heat broke out across my skin, sending me into a quick panic that perhaps I'm coming down with the flu and spiking a fever. Nothing has ever felt like this, especially not from a simple look from someone I can't even see.

Bringing my glass back up, I take another sip, keeping my gaze locked on him, not really sure what to do. Then he moves. He pushes off the wall, briefly turns to the woman standing at his side and says something that her body language can barely hide as she stiffens and then turns away from him. Long strides carry him across the room and my next breath stalls in my chest. Because he's walking right. To. Me.

Not only my next breath, but every ounce of air vanishes from the room as he stops in front of me. I have to manually remind myself to breathe before I tip my head back to look up at him, or his mask at least. Personal space apparently is not his thing, as the toes of his shoes nearly touch mine.

I'm going to hyperventilate.

Or pass out.

Or hyperventilate and *then* pass out.

The room goes fuzzy; a slow vignette encroaches my vision, and my hearing fades, morphing everyone's voice until only a faint buzzing remains. The world is gone, my focus only on him. Not a single word pierces the moment as he watches me, eyes pinging from my mask, down to my intentionally low dress. One wrong move and my tits would actually spill out of the fabric. It's too dark to tell the color of his eyes but they hover at my chest for a moment before sweeping along the slight dip in my waist and across my stomach. He lingers for another moment before dragging his gaze upward, back to me.

I don't know if any of it is good or bad.

Does he notice the soft, fullness of my stomach and is trying to find a polite way to turn around and go back to the leggy blonde he was with? Usually, if I'm in formal wear or anything tighter than jeans, there's some sort of compression layer to keep all of me in place but the least sexy thing you can do is peel off a pair of those, so I left them at home.

I even left my underwear at home, but that didn't seem like the best line to open up with.

Or maybe it is?

I have no idea what I should be doing right now.

Maxine appears at our side, from who knows where, probably sensing my oncoming panic. "Eros, I'm so glad you came tonight," she purrs, draping her hand on the man's shoulder with an effortless familiarity, "and how clandestine that you seem to be drawn to our very own Psyche."

"Psyche," he recites in a low voice.

"This is her first night here," Maxine offers. "I was hoping you two would cross paths."

I have to stop myself from asking her what she means but I bite my tongue instead.

The man, Eros, embraces Maxine, bending his head down to whisper something in her ear that makes her smile like the Cheshire Cat. "Of course, I'll have one of the staff members come get you when it's ready if she's agreed to join you."

Shifting on my feet, my eyes slide back and forth between them. What did he ask to get ready? Does Maxine mean me when she says if she agrees? He hasn't even said a single word to me. Does he think since I'm new here, I'm going to fall into bed with the first person to acknowledge me?

Better yet, why am I hoping she means me and why *am* I ready to fall into bed with the first guy to pay me any mind?

Maxine sashays away and his attention is back on me. "Psyche," he acknowledges again, lifting my free hand and, even though the mask is in the way, he places a faux kiss where my hand meets my wrist. Even his voice is attractive, it's deep and rich, like I've bitten into the decadent piece of chocolate cake. I may never see this man's face and yet, at this very moment, I would be perfectly content to only have him speak to me. As long as he continues speaking to me it would never even matter what he looks like.

"Hello," I manage to squeak out.

There's another quick tilt of his head, like he's trying to remember something before he speaks again. "And how is your first night?"

"Better now."

A dark chuckle comes from behind the mask at my response. "I like that."

Now it's my turn to question. "Like what?"

"A woman who says what's on her mind."

I almost scramble back and apologize, telling him actually I don't speak my mind but being here, in this dress, alright maybe it's the mask, is turning me into someone else. Someone I don't recognize but someone that I like.

Someone who gets exactly what they want.

Fuck it. Might as well give it my best shot and say whatever it is I want. "I think you'll find a lot of things about me you may like."

Eros' fingers tighten around my wrist, a simple twitch to remind me he never stopped touching me. The movement makes me want to crawl into his lap and feel his hands roam my body, see what it would be like to have them dig into the softness of all the parts I usually hate.

I'm trying to remember what I put down for public displays of affection when someone walks up to him, handing over what looks to be a set of keys. The gold ring slips around his finger before he pockets them.

Eros turns back to me. "If you haven't already committed to someone else, would you like to join me in my room?"

Desire pulls at my spine when he says the words. It wraps itself up each vertebrae until it reaches my throat, cutting off any chance of me answering. Instead I thread my fingers through his and give him a quick nod.

Eros leads me out of the main room, past the staircase and to the far side of the building. It looks like any other living room, and honestly a bit like the room in my grandmother's house where no one's really allowed to sit on any of the furniture. Except there is a couple occupying one of the couches. Or more so the man is on the couch with a woman sitting on him, faces millimeters apart with his hand sliding the strap of the woman's dress down as he kisses along her collarbone.

Before I intrude any further, I tear my eyes from them with a focus straight ahead as I'm led down a smaller hallway. "They like being watched," he says, pulling the keys from his pocket. "They can't do anything explicit in that room but they like to start there to draw in a crowd," he says while unlocking the door, answering a question I'm too shy to ask.

Before we walk through, he stops to turn to me. "Did you want to watch?"

Did I?

Moments pass but I'm not really contemplating his question. I'm frozen. I don't know how long I'm lost, until suddenly my hand is empty. Eros sweeps my dark curls back behind my shoulder, letting deft fingers trail along the slope of my neck and it pulls me back enough to answer. "No, thank you."

His chest swells with a deep breath. "So polite." The words are a whisper and the skin he's touching shudders.

I follow him into the room that looks almost like a standard hotel suite, equipped with a large four poster bed that looms in the middle of the room, with soft white bedding and so many pillows it's almost laughable. A chair sits in the corner facing the bed, a nightstand on one side and another doorway that, I'm guessing, leads to a bathroom. The only difference between here and the last hotel I checked into is a bookcase on the back wall near the bed, but instead of books, each shelf is dedicated to different types of toys.

To stop myself from blushing, I look away and walk toward the bed, running my hands along the bedding. I'm not quite sure what Egyptian cotton feels like, but this buttery soft duvet is probably exactly it.

Each breath comes out a bit more erratic than the last as I try my best to keep control. Until I see him reach for his mask. "Wait," I yell out, stalling his movement, startling even myself. "Do you think we can keep the masks on?"

It's a quick decision, one I didn't even know I was going to make. There's a real chance that if I saw what he actually looks like, I would spend the rest of my life looking for him in every crowd, and that's not what I want from this.

And as bad as it sounds, I really, really want to imagine a certain face in my head, which I can't do if I know what this man looks like. Maybe it makes me a terrible person but I can beat myself up about it later.

"Masks stay on," he agrees, eyes once again sweeping along my body. "Everything else comes off."

CHAPTER FIVE

Nolan

SHE ASKS FOR THE masks to stay on and I'm almost too quick to agree. Maybe it makes me an asshole, and maybe I'll have to answer for this at some point if pearly gates are in my future, but it would be worth it. If her mask stays on, it would make it that much easier to imagine *her*.

The moment I saw Psyche, my stomach hit the floor. Tunnel vision kicked in and she was all I saw. I don't even remember what the blonde was telling me when I left her but I was being pulled helplessly across the room by some invisible force.

Psyche's willowy cadence evokes a softness inside of me I associate with exactly one person. The one person I'm not allowed to have, the one person I know I would never see here, the one person I can never fully get out of my head. When Psyches speaks, it's as if Harper stands before me, but I know not to believe in wishful thinking.

Psyche. How ironic. Psyche is Eros' counterpart, his wife.

I never understood why Maxine insists on code names during these types of events or her insistent need to give everyone a nickname in general. She's done it for as long as I've known her. Maxine was the one to give me the name Eros, years ago when we first met while getting our MBA's, something about being from Cupid and looking the way I did. Two years in school was all we needed to solidify our friendship. We couldn't be more different but Maxine is my actual best friend. Nothing like the surface level friendship I have with Dan, one that only works if he's getting what he needs out of me and I get... Well, there's nothing I need from him so I guess it's a bit one sided.

For her fortieth birthday, I gave her enough start-up funds for Midnights, and my only caveat was I got a designated room. She was all too happy to oblige.

Psyche's fingers fiddle with the slit of her dress, with one arm crossing her body to hold onto the other. Nerves pouring out of her like rapid rivers.

"Psyche." Her head snaps to the sound of my voice and I suck in the urge to groan. I've been near her for all of two minutes and she's already everything I want.

Maxine has an affinity for women who like to test the boundaries she sets. I, however, prefer women who put their trust in me and know that with a little time, I will give them everything they crave.

"You're nervous."

She shifts in her heels and breathes out a laugh. "Am I that obvious?"

Crossing the room I make my way to her, planting myself in front of her in the same fashion as I did in the main room. "No, you're not, I just happen to be very good at noticing details." With very little effort, I sink to my knees before her and notice the quick change in her breath. "While I get you comfortable, why don't you tell me about yourself," I say, hoping maybe an exchange in details will help loosen her up. But when my fingers curl around her ankle, she stiffens. "It doesn't have to be anything personal, it can be anything you want."

She silently watches me through the openings of her mask but doesn't shrink out of my grasp when I slowly lift her foot and slip the strap out of the buckle around her ankle. The heel falls off her foot and I set it to the side.

Still not a word, so I do the same to the other and allow myself the simple pleasure of finally touching her soft skin.

"Thank you," she murmurs as I stand and watch her toes flex lightly against the hardwood floor. "What do you want to know?"

Circling around her, not unlike a hawk searching for prey, I don't answer until I'm at her back. "How about why you're here?" My fingers thread through the strands of her dark hair and Harper flashes through my mind. There's a special place in the pits of Hell for me, I'm sure of it, but I can't bring myself to care. I brush the silky locks to the side to expose the top of her zipper and I'm seconds away from dragging it down when she responds.

"I'm very"—she pauses for a second—"new to this."

My movements halt. I already know it's her first time here, so did she mean clubs in general, or God forbid—"New to sex?" I reluctantly question, trying my best to keep panic out of my voice. That is the last thing I need. I can teach a woman who is new to the club, but I don't know if I can teach a virgin. I can, but I don't know if I want to.

"What? No. I'm not a virgin I just meant experiences like this, the club, with a person I don't know and can't see. Things like that," she rushes to say.

Relief washes over me.

"Do you want to go through the list?" I ask, running the tips of my fingers along her shoulders.

She shakes her head. "I'm afraid I'm a little boring." Psyche turns her head to look at me through the mask. If I could see her, I'm sure a blush would be running across her cheeks.

"Impossible," I say, dragging my fingertips across her shoulder blades. Every featherlight touch darkens my vision until she is the only thing I see at the end of my tunnel vision. "What is it that you want?"

Psyche's heartbeat thuds against my finger tips continue to skate along her back and down her spine. Everything I'm made of, every molecule, every atom, wants to consume her until we're nothing but a tangled mess of limbs and sweat.

Through the mask the faint scent of jasmine envelopes me as her head drops back, resting against my shoulder as a deep sigh pushes from her chest. It's my favorite type of noise, heavy with want and the sense she's starving for my touch.

I repeat my question. "What do you want?"

"I-I don't know," she finally answers, and it's exactly what I'm hoping for.

Years of experience tell me her timid reply isn't just nervousness but an admission. No one automatically knows what they like in bed. It takes time, effort and the right partner to carve out the parts of ourselves we keep tucked away. Some people live their entire lives without figuring it out. It's one reason Maxine started Midnights.

"Can I show you what I think you'll like?" I whisper with my lips hovering near her ear.

Her nod is subtle but it's there.

"Are you on birth control?"

She shifts and nods again.

These are sexy questions but they're necessary.

"Would you prefer I wear a condom?" The words are clinical, but needed and I almost lose it when she whispers "no".

She's fucking perfect.

"You remember the safe word you were given?"

Everyone that comes into Midnights has one, and everyone's is the same to avoid any confusion. Psyche sucks in a breath as I toy with her zipper, waiting for her answer. "Olympus."

Maxine always did love her mythology references.

"Good. You hold all the power here. If you want to stop, at any point, all you have to do is say the word."

"Okay."

There's a howling urge to tear the dress from her body and fuck her into the mattress until she's nothing but a sobbing mess of pleasure. Eventually I'll get there, but she's as timid as a deer and would probably run if I lead with that.

Inch by inch, the teeth of the zipper part, exposing more of her skin until I hit the end and the flimsy fabric slinks to the floor with the slightest tug. Red pools at her feet and I think some sort of animalistic noise escapes me once she's bare. I'm not entirely sure because I am utterly captivated by her. Every thought in my head is replaced by her.

I want nothing but her.

I need nothing but her.

I desire nothing but her.

And it's unlike anything I've ever felt before. I've never been this affected by a woman, especially not one I've just met and one whose face I can't even see.

With steady steps I circle her like a vulture until we're standing in front of each other and the sound erupts from me again. This entire time, the only thing between us was her dress; underneath, she's completely bare. Not an inch of lace or frills, just her. Full tits, heavy with need, heave with each deep breath. Both adorned with rosy pink nipples that pebble into hardened points as I brush my fingers across them.

Her breathing picks up at my touch and her mouth drops in a loud gasp when I take one of the stiff peaks between my fingers in a light pinch.

"Eros," she breathes, and I suddenly wish she knew my name and the masks were gone. She would look phenomenal on her knees with my cock slipping between her lips. Fuck these masks suck. I won't be able to feel her lips on mine or bury my face between her legs to taste her.

Maybe I can ask her to come back? Maybe she'll want to see me again without them because I'm starting to realize how restricting they are.

So I tell her, because if I'm suffering, then I'm going to make sure she knows what she's missing. "Normally, I'd spend my time between these pretty thighs, eating until I've had my fill, but these masks would make that difficult."

My hand trails down her soft stomach until my hand cups her center. Warmth seeps into my palm and without thinking, her hips slant forward, searching for the pressure I know she wants.

I suppress a laugh. "What should I do with you instead?" I question but I'm already a goner, there's no use in holding back. Slipping my hand further between her thighs, I let my middle finger dip between her slit.

We've barely begun and yet she is already slick with arousal and there is little resistance as I let myself inside of her. Her legs part on their own, opening herself further. Enough for me to add another finger.

"Should I have you come on my hand right here in the middle of the room?" My fingers slowly plunge in and out of her as each breath catches on the one that follows. "Standing in front of me to use however I want?"

Pressing the heel of my hand against her clit forces a tangled cry from her. Behind the mask, I finally notice her eyes are a chocolate brown as they flash with need. Each stroke of my fingers quickly pulls her to the edge of her first orgasm. It's quicker than I expected but better than anything I could imagine.

I wonder how many times I can get her to come for me tonight? Not that it's a test, but four seems like a reasonable number.

Each passing second, she grows wetter, until my palm is slick with her. "Can you take one more angel?" I ask as

I place my free hand along her neck, my thumb pressing under her chin, forcing her to look at me.

"Yes, please," she whimpers.

That's all it took. That simple fucking word. I feel like I'm strapped onto a rocket about to be launched into space. I don't know what it is about that word but it twists my insides and makes me feel important. Like I'm the only one who can give this to her, something she desperately wants and is willing to even beg me for.

I add a third finger into her already tight channel and her pussy flutters around me. Clamping down and sucking me in as if it craves the stretch.

Psyche moans, guttural, raw and so fucking needy it makes my cock weep inside my pants.

I force her head to stay up and she keeps her eyes locked with mine as the room fills with the wet sounds of her as I pump in and out of her with a building pace.

When her thighs begin to tremble I know she's close. Her breathing picks up, stalling every few seconds when I curl and hit that spot inside of her that forces her eyes to squeeze shut.

"I think I'm going to—" she pants out.

"I know, Sweet Girl. Can you give me one right here?"

I'm not sure if she's registering me at all, as she loses herself in the moment.

"Eros, I'm going to..." Her sentence cuts off with silent scream as she falls off into an abyss of ecstasy.

I don't stop, I don't let up. She rides my hand without abandon, wildly bucking her hips as she cascades along with the climax tearing through her. A deep rose blush crawls across her chest and her hands latch onto my arms, fingers digging into my skin, and it's fucking beautiful.

After a moment, she drifts back down, and her body sags slightly but stays up right as I pull my hand from her.

Carefully, I lift the bottom of my mask just enough to slip my fingers underneath and pop them in my mouth. I don't think I could've stopped myself even if I wanted to. The need to have her taste on my tongue is powerful and too much for me to resist.

She tastes exactly like I want her to—musky, light, and all woman.

"You are unreal," I say as I unwillingly slip my fingers from my mouth. I invade her, pressing her chest against mine, I walk her backward until her knees hit the bed and then let her fall back.

"One down, but I need you to give me at least three more."

CHAPTER SIX

FEBRUARY 2

I'M WALKING ON CLOUD nine coming into work. I spent all of Sunday swathed in a cocoon of bliss, and zero thoughts about work or the upcoming week or even the Cupid Ball. I can't remember the last time I took a Sunday—or any day, for that matter—to myself.

Multiple orgasms apparently seem to be the secret to a soft life. Someone should alert the news outlets.

There's only one thing threatening to pop my perfect bubble, one thought lingering in the back of my head—he hasn't texted me. Not that I'm waiting around for the moment his name appears on my screen. He was so insistent on exchanging numbers that I just assumed I would hear from him soon, but nothing.

With the sun still fighting to peek above the horizon, I slide into my desk to start the day. The office is always quiet this early in the morning, perfect to leisurely scroll through emails. Within twenty minutes, I reach the bottom of my inbox, there's a soft stream of sunlight filtering in, and my coffee has gone from scolding to perfect. Maybe this week won't be so bad, regardless if Eros has called or not.

My computer chimes, and when I glance at the incoming email, I recognize the sender immediately. I'm not superstitious; I'll step on a crack, walk under a ladder, and I couldn't care less if I break a mirror, but maybe I should reconsider. One thought about everything working in my favor and now I've been kicked head first into jinxing myself.

Cupids' Charity Ball is in less than two weeks, and while I may have slacked off on some of my duties, I booked the vendors months ago. So why is Veronica from Party Rental

Express emailing me over the weekend with the subject line *Phone Call Request*?

My teeth clamp down on my bottom lip as a lead weight drops in my stomach when I pull open the email.

"Oh no," I finally say into the emptiness that is my office. "No, no, no."

One perfect weekend ruined by an email. It's barely eight in the morning, but I immediately pick up the phone. Crossing my fingers as if the small act holds some magical power over party orders, I wait for her to answer. With each ring, my mind spirals further out of control until I feel the beginning prick of tears behind my eyes. Luckily, Veronica answers before I do anything rash, like actually cry when I don't even have all the facts.

"Hi, Veronica, it's Harper from Cupid. I know it's early but I got your email and wanted to touch base."

She sighs into the receiver. Not a good sign, maybe I was right to start crying. "Hi, Harper. I'm so sorry to do this. When you booked, I was out on maternity leave and the temp they brought in as my backup booked all your rentals when they were already assigned to another event."

"Which ones?" I grip the phone until there's a slight crack of the plastic.

"All of them."

The air rushes from my lungs as I register the worst possible outcome. "Please tell me you're joking. Everything we picked is the same?"

"I'm afraid so, both events are Valentine themed and apparently you guys have the same taste. I'm so sorry, Harper."

I know this isn't her fault, but I want to scream. "It's okay," I say instead.

"I can give you some leads for other companies but they're all in the Bay, and with Valentine's Day on a Saturday this year, there's a lot of parties that weekend."

What she's saying is I'll need a Hail Mary to find somewhere with the items I need.

"Okay, thanks, Veronica."

Her email with the list, a small list, I might add, must have already been drafted because not even a minute later, my computer pings with the incoming message.

My plans for the morning are now out the window. The Cupid Ball is a town staple, it's what we're known for across the county. The amount of money it brings in sustains some departments' budgets for the entire year, and I don't even want to think about what would happen if I have to cancel. And if I have to tell my father the Ball is canceled because of rentals, I might as well kiss my job goodbye.

I can't prove my dad hates that I work in the same building as him, despite him getting me this job, but it sure feels like it. There hasn't been a single report I've sent to his inbox that he hasn't sent back with some sort of note about revisions being needed. Ridiculous revisions at that—like the shade of red on a cover page is too dark, or he wants pie-charts instead of bar graphs. I change them, of course, but each time he does it, a little piece of me withers up inside. And he hates when people figure out I'm his daughter. His *other* daughter he always likes to interject with.

Parents shouldn't play favorites but we all know they do. Ask any middle child and they'd all agree on how easily we're overlooked. But to my parents, I'm not just the middle child, I'm the less than perfect child, the child who doesn't fit the image of their idea of a perfect family. The "one boy, one girl, has a Labrador Retriever and house in the 'burbs" type of image.

No, I'm the child who didn't come out a boy. I pursued an arts degree instead of business. I've been labeled overweight since before I knew what it meant. I always have been and always will be less than, and even if I give up trying to be a part of the family, there is still a part of me that doesn't want to give more fuel to hate me. And canceling his beloved event would only add to an already raging fire.

It took me the entire morning but I finally found one rental place that has *almost* everything I originally booked. They were out of red table runners but I'm nothing if not resourceful and can easily sew two dozen myself in ten days.

All of that would be great if we didn't have to pay almost double the original quote.

Which means I need Nolan's approval.

I've been standing on the other side of his closed door for at least five minutes, searching for the courage to go in but it keeps slipping through my fingers. Where is the girl from this weekend, the one who spoke up for herself? I could really use her right about now.

Sadie tsks from behind me. "You can go in, you know? He's not in a meeting."

"I know, Sadie," my annoyance loud and clear.

With my hand raised, I'm halfway to knocking when my phone chimes and being saved by the bell has never felt better. Sadie watches with a confused look on her face as I back out of the room, balancing reports in one hand and digging for my phone with the other.

"I'll be right back," I say to her, not that she cares.

I need to see you again.

What happened to hello?

That's what I should say but I don't. Seeing his words mirror my thoughts sends sparks flying across my skin, lighting up every nerve ending I have and washing me in a sense of relief. I was beginning to think he only asked for my number out of some weird sense of chivalry. You know... *I came inside you, made you come multiple times, why not get your number so it doesn't feel cheap*, sort of thinking.

I'd like that very much.

His next text appears before I finish my message.

Tomorrow. Midnights at 8:00

Something about the urgency in his text stokes the kindling on the pleasure leftover from the weekend, but there's no way he thinks I'm a member and can return. I remember Maxine telling him I was there as part of the open house. At no point was I ever going to become a member, I work in local government. Small town government at that, I barely make the monthly dues in six months. I was there for the experience, he knew that.

> I'm not a member at Midnights

His next text takes a bit longer but when it comes I have to bite my lip to keep from squealing.

> It's been taken care of. Tomorrow at 8:00.

> I'll be there

> And no masks this time. I have to see you.

I've been actively trying to think about what's behind his golden armor. Now that it's a possibility my skin starts to buzz.

> Yes, Sir

I don't wait for his reply as I shove my phone into my pocket and stride back toward Nolan's door. Knocking twice and I push through with a new wave of confidence. My knees falter at the sight of him smiling down at his phone.

Nolan never smiles. But here he is mid-morning on a Monday grinning at his phone like a kid who's about to be set loose in a candy shop. He only notices I'm standing in front of him after I clear my throat. His smile drops when he looks up. He sets his phone down and now I'm facing the detached and stoic man I'm used to seeing.

"Morning, Harper," he greets, shifting his seat to roll closer into the desk. "How can I help you?"

I've got this. He can't really say no and it's not like it's my fault anyway. "There was an issue with the rental company for the Cupid Ball. Apparently they double booked their stock and have canceled our order." I'm ready with the solution and research to prove the twice-as-expensive vendor is the only option, but the way he's staring at me has all my hard work and well thought out monologue jumbled in my head.

His gaze is piercing and attentive. I have to take a second to remind myself to breathe.

"I found a company that has almost everything we booked with the exception of the table runners, but I'll take care of those personally."

"Why do I sense another 'but' coming?"

"Because there is," I reply.

The words seem to be stuck in my chest. Absent-mindedly, I tug on the plain gold necklace I have on, pulling the charm back and forth. Nolan's eyes lock onto the movement. He watches me with an almost feline interest.

I can't help myself. "It's double the price," I say as I release the charm and slowly drag the tips of my fingers down my chest, running along the hint of cleavage I risked showing today.

Damn, maybe Midnights is worth the monthly fee if one night gave me the confidence to try and use my body to get my boss to spend money I know the town doesn't have. It's not the worst thing in the world, right? I'm sure there are government officials out there using their influence to get things much seedier than dinnerware for a party. Actually I know there are.

My hand falls to my lap, not willing to risk anything more. But he's still watching me, fingers now pressing against his soft lips—I really hope it isn't because he's holding in a laugh. But I don't think he is. Mankind, or rather men, has set the bar practically in Hell. Add in being exposed to men like my father and his friends at an early age, I'm feel as if I'm always waiting for the punchline to come at my expense. But with Nolan, I've never heard a negative word about me, or women in general, leave his mouth. He's also the best looking of my father's friends, which doesn't hurt either.

"Nolan."

He shakes his head free of whatever vortex he's stuck in. "Sorry." A look roams across his face for a moment as our eyes meet before he tears away from me. "It's not a problem, make sure they send the invoice today and you can pay it."

That's it? My arsenal is chock full of arguments to get this done and I don't have to use any of them?

"And you're okay with the extra cost eating into basically the whole budget for the recreation department for this month and next?"

He leans into the tilt of his chair and slips his hand behind himself. He brings his hand back out with his wallet, slips out a shiny black card and slides it in front of me. "Just put it on my card and I'll fix the budgets."

Now I'm more confused than anything.

"Isn't this... I don't know, collusion, or something?"

His smile returns. "I think they care more about using government funds to pay for personal expenses, not the other way around."

The card is heavy in my hand, clearly made of metal and a limit so high it'd be impossible to max out, if there was a limit at all. "Are you sure about this?"

"We both know your dad would make it your problem."

"Since when do you care about my problems?" The question slips out before I can stop it. If only a hole would open and swallow me whole right now, save me from my own embarrassment.

The scowl I always assumed was a permanent fixture on Nolan's face softens. "Is that what you think of me? That I don't care about you?"

I force myself to look at him and not at my hands twisting around in my lap. "Well, yeah, because why would you? You may be my dad's friend, but you don't know me. You've never taken the time to talk to me outside of making sure I send in reports, and the few times I've been at my parents the same time as you, you never acknowledge me. You stare at me, but you don't talk to me."

Stillness falls around the office. My words hang in the air. It sounds desperate, and I don't want to be that woman. I don't want Nolan to know how much it bothers me to be ignored by him. And I don't *want* to want him. Especially now that Eros is in the picture.

But I do.

"I didn't realize you noticed." His voice is painfully low but I heard him.

"I—"

The office door swings open and my father's voice precedes him. "Nolan, Sandy and I are having a dinner party tomorrow night. I've invited the mayors from Fairvale and Cornelia and I need you to be there," my father commands, barely registering I'm here. "And oh—Harper you're here."

"I was just leaving." My voice lacked any warmth I used to possess for him, the part that yearned for my father's affection died a long time ago.

He doesn't notice, he never does. "Your mother would've invited you but it's very last minute, you understand."

"Don't worry about it. I have plans tomorrow night anyway."

He looks all too pleased that I won't be tainting his perfect dinner party. I can't even remember the last time my parents asked me to dinner and not as an after thought.

Standing from my chair, I swipe the card from the table while my father is fiddling with his tie. "Thank you, Mr. Archer. I'll be done and have this back to you soon," I say, almost robotic.

Nolan's eyes leave scorch marks in my back as I leave, making me feel almost guilty for going to see Eros tomorrow.

But why?

I'm not tied to anyone, I'm free to see whomever I want, whenever I want. So why does one soft look from Nolan, and one single hint that I'm not just some employee, or his friend's daughter, send me into some sort of sexual crisis mode?

CHAPTER SEVEN

FEBRUARY 3

MY SECOND DRIVE TO Midnights is less sweaty. Which is great for my make up, but the nerves were still plucking at my system. Meeting Eros without our masks feels more daunting than choosing to come to a sex club in the first place. Almost as if it's more real somehow.

A couple exits their car at the same time as I do. The woman offers me a polite smile before taking her partner's hand, confidently strolling toward the building. One tiny, simple gesture and an ache rolls through my gut. Even though I know it shouldn't. Weren't we all here for the same reason? If anything, I should feel more at ease, but my walk to the entrance is done slowly, with my thumbs nervously flicking along my fingertips.

At least the bouncer is a familiar face. Even if it's still as stoic with zero hint that he recognizes me. "Name?" he asks, clearly focused on getting people inside and nothing else. When I give him my name, and he doesn't turn me away, my breathing becomes lighter.

But the relief is short-lived. I have no idea what Eros looks like. All I know is he has dark hair, and looking around more than half of these men fit the criteria. I'm not even sure if any random person would know his code name. I definitely didn't ask enough questions before agreeing to this.

This is one time I wish I were more outgoing, maybe more like my sister, able to command any room I walk into. But instead, I slide toward the first empty space I spot and wait for...well I don't really know who. That's my whole problem but melting into the wall is not the way to get noticed by a man who doesn't know what I look like but it's the only thing that feels right.

My saving grace comes in the form of a smiling Maxine. She walks directly toward me, politely greeting a few people as she moves through the crowd. Tonight, she's in black again, but a jaw dropping two piece fitted suit that glistens with each step, thousands of stars sewn directly into the fabric. Her jacket hangs open and underneath is only a matching bra that sits against her deep olive toned skin.

"Psyche," she greets, bending to kiss me quickly on each cheek like she would an old friend.

Clumsily bumping against her cheek, I return the gesture and fumble over a simple hello. For some reason I didn't expect her to remember me. Maxine saw guests every night and while this is only my second night, she acts as if I'm a member she sees regularly. Probably why this place is so successful. If you can make even the most timid of people feel welcome and secure in an environment, then they'll be more willing to come back.

Although the use of the code name she gave me last time was unexpected. I lean in and ask, "I'm sorry, but are we supposed to use those names still? I thought it was only for the open house."

Her ruby red lips part in a laugh. "You don't have to, but I think it suits you."

I'm choosing to ignore the unknown meaning in her words. Maxine steps out of my view, and I expect her to walk off and mingle with the rest of her guests, but I'm surprised as she shifts to stand at my side.

"Everyone you see here started out just like you."

My head turns to look at her, "What do you mean?"

"You're nervous."

"So everyone keeps saying."

She laughs again. "One night here doesn't make anyone an expert. It usually takes quite a few times before someone walks in here confidently."

"How long did it take you? Assuming your business isn't the first club you've been to."

"You assume correctly," she answers before pondering my question for a moment. "I come from a very religious family where sex is not only not talked about but is viewed as something married couples are expected to do to produce children and that's it. It wasn't until I was in my early thirties that I started to explore my sexuality *and* sensuality. Then it was a long time after that when I became really comfortable with who I was."

Looking at the woman next to me, I would think she was always like this; strong, commanding, exuding the type of confidence people search their whole lives for. It's humbling to know how similar we may be.

I sigh and look back at the crowd. "My family isn't religious, I fear my hesitation is purely internalized. Like I shouldn't want to *want* to be here."

Maxine looks over at me, even in my heels, she still has to look down slightly. Dark eyes study me as a soft smile plays at her lips. "As long as it's what *you* want. That's the beauty of all of this." She waves around the room. "We can be whoever we want."

A nervous laugh expels past my lips. "You make it sound so easy."

She leans over and whispers, "It can be."

Who am I to argue with an expert?

We spend the next minute in silence, people watching before she speaks again. "Eros should be here soon and asked me to show you to his room."

At the mention of his name, my heart skips and my stomach clenches. Standing around with Maxine, I almost forgot about him.

Almost.

Maxine slips her hand into mine and I follow her through the main room. A few people stop and watch us, their eyes jumping between our faces and where our hands are joined with a longing look. Not necessarily jealous but

I got the impression from a few of the people we passed, men and women, that they would do anything to be the person Maxine was leading back to the rooms.

It makes me curious about what she might be like behind closed doors. To command that type of attention, fully clothed, would make me dizzy I think, but she was made for it.

We walk a familiar short path and she unlocks the same door and allows me to enter past her. "Thank you, Maxine," I say, hoping she knows it's for more than just showing me to the room. Every time I talk to her, it ends up a bit deeper than I intend but she never makes me feel like I'm intruding.

"You're so welcome, Psyche. Have a good night." She pulls the door closed behind her.

Alone in the room, my heartbeat begins to take off at a rapid pace. With no mask to hide behind, I suddenly feel more exposed than I expected.

What if he walks in and hates what he sees? What if our last time together was a fluke? What if the mask gave me more confidence than I really possess and tonight ends up one huge disappointment?

What if he's ugly?

I'm not a shallow person, or at least not more than the average person, but I don't know if I would be able to finish if I'm looking at someone who I don't find attractive. No matter how good his cock is.

Okay, maybe that did make me shallow.

I need to get it together, before I start spiraling.

I move to the bathroom to give myself a final once over. It's not the dress from the open house but it's as tight, and even shorter, hugging the tops of my thighs. One slight bend and everything would be on display, which is kind of the point. Pulling off the long coat I wore over the top for that exact reason, I toss it to the side and lean closer toward the mirror.

Makeup is still in place, hair still full of curls.

The faint sound of the doorknob turning catches my attention. Butterflies take flight in my stomach.

A creak of the door. Flames erupt under my skin.

Heavy footsteps approach behind me. Euphoria trickles through my veins in anticipation.

"Psyche," Eros' deep timber voice calls out.

I can't see him in the mirror but he's here. He's here, and every ounce of hesitation evaporates.

"Eros," I call out, quickly turning around, stepping out of the bathroom, meeting him face-to-face.

Except Eros isn't looking back at me.

A shrill scream barrels out of me. I turn and flee back into the safety of the bathroom.

CHAPTER EIGHT

It's Harper.

Harper is standing in front of me.

Or she was until she screamed and locked herself in the bathroom.

For some reason, I look over my shoulder at the door I walked through, thinking maybe it turned into some type of portal. That's the only logical explanation for my dreams to manifest right before my eyes.

I came for Psyche, who's wedged herself in between every one of my thoughts and yet Harper is the one who is here. Harper, my every thought.

Maybe I've died and this is Heaven.

An atom bomb detonates in my head at the realization.

Psyche is Harper.

Fuck that means the woman who came on my hand, whose taste seared my tongue, and legs wrapped around my waist while taking every inch I gave her was Harper. My employee. My friend's daughter.

I clear my throat. "Harper?" I call out her name, sounding foreign while in this room.

Nothing happens. Gently knocking on the door. I call out her name again and I wait until she slowly pulls the door open.

"Oh, god, it is you," she groans, pushing past me, stalking into the room.

My eyes follow her, committing every part of her to memory. Thighs I dream about getting my face in-between, tits I want to slide my cock between, an ass I want to—basically anywhere Harper will let me near with my mouth, hands, or dick is somewhere I want to be. If she'll let me, but right now she looks as if she wants me to disappear. Probably off the planet entirely, if she got her way.

She paces across the room, chewing on her thumb refusing to look at me.

"What are you doing here?" I demand.

Nolan, you fucking idiot.

She doesn't need to be accused, she needs reassurance.

Her eyes snap to me, kindling igniting in her gaze. "Me? What are *you* doing here?" She violently shakes her head, as if the movement will erase me from her sight. "You know what, never mind." Harper snatches a coat from the chair and dashes out the door.

For a second I think about not following her but there's a much bigger devil on my shoulder that wins. But before I follow, I swipe a folder off the table.

Will Maxine rip me a new one when she finds out—yes, but we didn't go over the list our first night and I have to know what brought her to Midnights.

Harper's fighting her way through the crowd ahead of me. Someone shouts her name, but she doesn't stop and keeps pushing her way to the front door.

I turn to see who is calling after her, only to see Maxine with a look of worry on her face. She follows the line Harper left with her eyes, which leads to me. "So that didn't go well." She says.

"No, it didn't, I—" That makes me stop. I turn to Maxine. "Wait, what?"

"There was a fifty-fifty chance she would either run out of the building, or run into your arms. Just so you know, I was rooting for the latter."

"What the fuck, Maxine? What are you talking about?"

"You thought I wouldn't look up the one woman you can't stop talking about?"

My neck cranes in time to see Harper walk out the front door. Maxine looks pleased with herself but I only have time for one revelation tonight. "We're not done." I point the folder at her and rush past people as she shouts, reminding me I'm not allowed to take it from the premises.

By the time I get outside, she is darting toward the parking lot. It only takes me a few seconds to catch up with her.

"Harper, please wait," I bellow into the night.

"No thank you!" she shouts over her shoulder, steps away from her car. I break into a jog to get to her before she gets in and leaves me in the dust.

My hand comes down on the door handle as she yanks it open.

"Nolan, please do not make this any more embarrassing than it is."

"This isn't embarrassing, this is..."

"A nightmare?" she blurts out as I say, "Unexpected."

When she pauses, everything comes to a halt around us and for a moment, we just stare at each other, like figures in a snow globe. Harper swallows loudly, stealing little glances at me. "You're not horrified, it's…me?"

I hate the way the word drips out of her mouth, like it's an unfathomable notion. The single syllable breaks whatever resolve I have in me because I can't stand the fact that she has no idea how I feel about her.

In the six months I've worked with Harper, I've slowly let myself spiral down a hole where I'm consumed by her. Not a single thought passes through my head that I don't automatically look for a way to tie to her. When I'm dressing for the day, I wonder which suit she would like best. On my drive into town, I run through my tasks for the day and see which of them will bring me in contact with her and then make those a priority. At night when I'm home alone, I fantasize about having her across the counter from me while I cook and yearn to know what she likes best. And at night, I fall into bed only to fuck my own fist at the thought of her.

Harper lives in the crevices of my brain and yet I've also spent the last six months trying to get her out because everything tells me we could never be together. There are so many reasons to choose from that I'm left paralyzed.

A twenty year age gap, the fact I'm her boss, and her dad has been my friend since we were children. Take your pick, any one of those will pull in gossip and snide remarks from everyone in Cupid, guaranteed, and that's not what I want for her. Not to mention I frequent Midnights because my tastes in bed extend past what I can get from simple hook ups.

I'm not the type of man who deserves a woman like Harper, but that doesn't stop me from wanting her.

"Horrified isn't even on the spectrum of my feelings."

She finally looks at me and the weak tie holding back my secret longing for her comes undone. Brown eyes, darker than then night sky and more captivating than anything I'll ever encounter stare back at me, pulling me in like a siren. It's a certain death for me if I follow her but I'm not sure a sweeter way to go exists.

Don't do it. Don't do it.

Just leave her, I try to convince myself. I can live the rest of my life without corrupting her. For once I wish I was the type of man I am in the bedroom. The type of man who likes to give, who isn't selfish, but I'm not.

"You said you wanted to learn, to explore your sexuality with a partner."

She groans and buries her face into her hands, trying to hide. "Don't remind me. God I'm so embarrassed you saw me like that."

I step closer and already dizzy thinking about everything I can show her. With a soft tug around her wrist, I pull her hands down but she's avoiding me again. I can't stand it.

"Harper, look at me." My voice is gentle but the command is there and I wait to see how she responds.

Her chest fills with a deep breath and once she exhales she slowly lifts her head. A beast in my chest unfurls, threatening to strut around at the simple act of obedience and it's hard not to let him loose.

"Beautiful," I praise and watch as she stands up a little straighter.

Now the beast struts around.

"If you want to pretend like this never happened, I can do that. We'll show up for work tomorrow and it will be like any other day, or—" I pause, waiting to see how she'll respond or if my attempt is futile.

It's a small movement but hard not to miss when her tongue darts out to wet her bottom lip before replying in a soft voice. "Or what?" It's not a threat, it's an opening.

"Or I can show you anything, everything, you want to learn."

The weighted statement rolls across her face as we stand in the near dark. There haven't been many people out here but a few pass us, saying nothing on their way inside. Frigid air blows around us as Harper pulls the thick jacket tighter around her. Any more lingering and I'm going to have to convince her to go back inside before the tip of her nose turns pink.

"I don't know if I can be with you...in there."

A breath whooshes past my lips. At least she didn't end the sentence where I thought she was going to. "Would you be more comfortable in my home?"

"Maybe?" she questions. "I'm not sure what to think right now, it's all a bit...much."

"Of course but you'll think about it?"

She nods and the beast roars.

"That's all the hope I need."

She doesn't say another word until she opens up her car door and slips into the driver's side. "You'd really be okay with teaching me?" she asks, staring out the windshield, gripping the wheel until her knuckles turn ghost white.

God, I want nothing more than to rip the clothes from her body, bury my face between her legs, and show her just how okay I am with it. Instead, with quick precision, I duck my upper body into her car. A surprised noise squeaks out of Harper.

She smells good, it's like being spun in a cotton candy machine when I'm near her. But that's Harper, she's everything soft, light, and sweet in this world.

About a month after I started as City Manager, when I was still boiling in my bitterness from being exiled back to Cupid, there was an elementary school class visiting. Why third graders want to know about local government is beyond me, but the place was overrun with children, some screaming, a couple crying and in general all around chaos. We were all miserable, every single employee. Hell, even the teacher looked like she was two minutes from leaving the kids and walking out—everyone, but Harper.

That was the first time I *noticed* Harper. She was calm, empathetic with the children and possessed the type of kindness the world needs more of. Before that day, my list of what attracted me to Harper was purely superficial. All of which are still correct, but after that day the list grew, and I started paying more attention to who Harper is and not just what she looks like.

I drag my nose up the column of her throat, inhaling until I'm drowning in sugar, and my lips hover at her ear. "I've been dreaming of you in my bed and I'll be in agony until you give me your answer, Sweet Girl."

I press a kiss against her cheek and only linger for a moment before telling her goodnight and shutting her car door.

If I'm going to Hell, at least I'll have earned my place.

CHAPTER NINE

FEBRUARY 4

THE LAST HOUR OF the day was slowly dwindling, and I deserve a gold medal for how well I've done, spending every hour hyperaware of Nolan's every movement, ensuring to be wherever he's not after reluctantly showing up for work. I didn't sleep last night. Not a single second.

Every quiet passing minute was an elusive reprieve from the white hot embarrassment still coursing through me.

I even swallowed my pride enough to go through Sadie the one time I needed something from him. It's not that I don't want to see him; the exact opposite, actually. More so, my problem is I'm afraid of running into him in the middle of City Hall and blurting out 'yes, please teach me everything you know about sex' because when's the last time desperation turned someone on?

Never, probably, and I'm not about to test the theory.

There's also still a chance I'll change my mind and pretend like last night never happened. It might be what's best because I still can't wrap my mind around him wanting me when a man like him can have anyone is beyond my comprehension. That's not even a self loathing statement, it's the truth. He could have movie stars, models, heirs to obscure royal thrones—literally anyone.

The Archer family may have started out as a small band of settlers, but that was two hundred years ago. Fast forward to today and their family is worth hundreds of millions, thanks to expanding railroads through the Central Valley. There's not a household in California that doesn't know the Archer name.

His money may intimidate me but everything else is nothing. Two decades is no small amount, you can live multiple lives within that span of time, but it doesn't bother me. Our age difference is one of the bigger incentives. I want to learn, and there's no better way to do that than with someone who has years of experience.

The fact he's my dad's best friend isn't my favorite fact but it's not like we're screaming for people to look at us. This is strictly a private, even secret, relationship. If my dad ever found out, I'm not sure I would ever recover from the fallout. I can hear his words now, he would find some way to blame me, that I somehow seduced him, because God forbid someone from their world would want someone like me.

Typing out one last quick email, the clock finally ticks to four. Relief and disappointment swirl around in my chest. Maybe it's better this way. Besides the one night we shared, we have nothing in common.

Yes, I'm sure this is for the best and I need to move on. The amount of emotional whiplash, from wanting him to telling myself I don't want him is exhausting.

It's probably time I re-start my job search anyway, a much better use of my time. I've been stuck in Cupid for two years since failing out of my first art docent job and running back to a town that never gave me anything. This is the exact kick in the pants I need to leave again.

Silently I vow to myself to update my resume as I race through packing up to leave, shoving anything my hand touches into my bag. Walking out of my office with my head hanging low, I smack into the one man I'm resolving to never think about again.

"Leaving?" he questions with a tilt of his head.

My eyes flutter, and I inhale deeply. God, he smells good, and my mind races back to the last time I was pressed into his body, wrapped in his scent. This is the exact opposite of what I want to focus on.

"I leave at the same time every day." I do my best to keep my voice steady and nonchalant.

"Yes, I know. That's why I'm here." He casts his gaze down at me. "Can you be at my house around seven tonight?"

"Your house?"

"Yes."

My mouth hangs open but nothing comes out.

Nolan's voice drops to a whisper. "Unless you want to go with the first option?"

Saying no to him is an option, he made that abundantly clear. I have all the power here. All it would take is a simple utterance of the word 'no' and we can resume being whatever it is we were before. Coworkers, I guess.

He can go back to acting like I barely exist, and I can go back to whatever sad version of me existed before Midnights.

I have the power to call this off before it ever really begins.

But it's not a power I want to wield.

"I need your address."

A smirk takes over his face, brightening the drab government office walls and like I've stepped onto a sunny beach. He pulls his phone out and seconds later mine pings with the location.

"Seven o'clock," he says again, and I nod. "You won't regret this, Harper, I promise."

I know I won't, that's part of the problem.

Cupid is the size of a thimble. Half the time I can't even pump gas without running into my elementary school teacher and my ex-boyfriend's mom from eighth grade. Which means my oversized coat and baseball cap are warranted, even for the drive to the outskirts of town. God forbid, an Archer actually lives in the town they founded.

I've never been to Nolan's house, there's never been a reason for me to, but I didn't expect to pull up to what appears to be some sort of ranch style house on a vast amount of empty land after driving twenty minutes out of town. Cute doesn't seem like a word Nolan would want used when describing his home, but I'm calling it like I see it. I park next to his sleek black Audi after coming to the head of his endless driveway.

A porch wraps around the entire perimeter of the house and baskets of flowers hang from top railings every few feet. He even has matching oak rocking chairs near the far corner looking out to where the sun would set. I'm walking into my dream home and he doesn't even know it.

But despite the allure of the world's most perfect house, there's a tiny, tiny voice jumping around for attention, telling me this might be the worst idea I've ever had. The video application comes into a smooth number two spot since it's what caused this whole thing.

Night air whistles through the open space and my chest starts to burn with a scratchy sort of sensation. Maybe this is a trick. Maybe he's really my father's friend through and through and has devised a whole elaborate 'I want to teach you sex things' situation in order to embarrass me to a high heaven so I finally leave this town for good.

A quick retreat is what I need to do. I'm barely on the stairs, there's still time to leave. I can simply tell him I've decided on the first option and pretend our one night never happened. It might just be the hardest thing I'll ever do, but I can do it.

That sounds like the perfect plan, I'll tell him I changed my mind and start looking for a new job far, far away from Cupid, maybe away from Northern California altogether.

I hear Denmark's a great place to live.

But as I finally work up the courage to take my first step backward, the door is yanked open. "Sorry, sorry, sorry. I had the music on while I was cooking and didn't hear your car." Nolan's words rush out in a tangled mess, opening the door wider and motioning for me to come in.

My steps are hesitant because what in the body snatchers is going on? I'm wracking my brain for the last memory I have of him apologizing, but everything comes up blank. Not only is he apologizing but the words seem to be sincere.

I avoid eye contact as I enter his home. Nolan peels my jacket from my shoulders without a word, and I turn to see him gingerly hang up my thrift store find next to what I know for a fact is a five hundred dollar suit jacket.

Everything about us is the opposite. We're two ends of a spectrum that's as wide as the universe.

He motions me forward and I follow without thought until we reach the kitchen. Every inch of his place is immaculate and inviting. All warm tones and a sense that he takes a lot of pride in his space.

The stove is overflowing with pans as a heavenly smell of garlic sauce fills the air. "I hope you're hungry," Nolan says, as if he can hear my stomach growl.

Popping myself up onto a barstool, I answer, "Starving, I didn't eat much today."

Nolan sets a bowl in front of me. "Well we can't have that now, can we?"

A blush creeps across my chest but I don't answer. Instead I look across the vast kitchen island to where he's standing, still partially in his suit. The dark Oxford button down with the top two buttons popped open, sleeves cuffed and rolled to his elbows. But what intrigues me the most is the hint of a smile playing at the corner of his mouth. As if he's fighting the urge to split into a full grin.

It strikes me as curious because this is not the man I'm accustomed to. The Nolan I know is stark, a man who lives in black and white with no room for gray or anything that isn't cut and dry. A man who doesn't participate in anything at work that requires him to mingle. A man whose mere presence commands attention and respect when he walks into a room. The type of person you step to the side for because getting in his way just isn't an option.

Nolan has always placed himself on the highest shelf, unattainable to everyone but none of that exists right now.

Tearing my gaze from the hold he has on me, I do the only other thing I can and start eating.

Of course, even his food is fantastic.

Nolan watches and finally the smile he is holding back breaks and takes over his face. That's all it takes. I definitely made the right decision.

CHAPTER
TEN

Nolan

TEN SQUARE FEET SEPARATE us, that's it. The length of my kitchen island but I might as well be wandering through the Sahara. Harper's here though, sitting in front of me, in a seat I've imagined her in a thousand times, so that has to account for something. Maybe she's simply curious or maybe, just maybe, she's really here for what we both want.

The last thing I want to do is pressure her, but the easiest way to loosen someone up is food and the bowl I placed in front of her is nearly empty. "That was great. Normally I don't eat pasta but this was really good." Harper sings my praises.

"I know."

"You know what?" The words come out a bit garbled as she sucks up a rouge strand of spaghetti.

"You do eat pasta, you just don't eat pasta with sauce."

She blinks, staring at me like six heads have sprouted in the span of a few seconds and cocks her head to the side. "How do you know that?" Harper shakes her head. "Actually, better question, why do you know that?"

An internal war breaks out. Do I tell her exactly how long she's been in my head? If I do, it might send her running again. I shouldn't, I know I shouldn't, but the beast is back, frantically pacing in my chest.

Fuck it.

What I want isn't fair unless I also bear myself completely to her.

I'm not a man of many words, but I am a man of action with a keen sense of observation. I've watched Harper, studied her.

Harper's a work of art that should be displayed in the Louvre. The type of painting people travel across the world for even a glimpse. I spend hours looking at her and each minute I find something new to fixate upon. Like the one soft brown freckle on the side of her mouth or the one tendril of hair at the nape of her neck that naturally spirals into the perfect ringlet.

I notice more about Harper than I should but who can blame me?

"I notice everything about you. From the fact you prefer all your food plain, or how when you're really focused or concentrating on work, you stick your tongue out. At work, you wear heels but only on Mondays and Fridays. You are on more social committees than I knew existed because you love people. You hang renaissance artwork in your office, and when people ask you why, you tell them no real reason, just that you like it. But I think it's because you miss working at the museum, so you surround yourself with pieces you miss the most."

"Oh," she whispers.

"I see you, Harper. I see you more than anyone else."

Her mouth parts and her next breath is ragged. "I lied to you," she says suddenly.

I straighten up. Those are never good words. "About what?"

"Well kind of lied. At Midnights." Her words are shaky, teeth gnawing at her plush bottom lip. "If we're going to do this I want to make sure you know what you're getting into. And after that display of...well, I don't know what, but I feel like I lied to you."

I wait as she fidgets in her chair, mumbling something under her breath.

"Harper, I can't hear you." I said gently.

She inhales deeply. "I have zero experience with any of this."

Silence drops over us, only a slight hum fills the room.

"But you said you weren't a virgin?" Now I'm getting nervous. It wouldn't change my answer, not now, I'm in this, but it would change some aspects.

"I'm not." She pauses for far longer than I expected. "Technically."

"Technically, you're not a virgin. I'm not sure what that's supposed to mean."

"It means I've had sex but before the other night it had been a while since I had even done that."

"Define awhile."

"Years," she says, almost like a question.

"You're joking."

"I'm not."

My hands press into the countertop as I lean in. "But how?"

"Do you really want me to sit here and tell you all the ways men don't see me or when they do, it usually ends with them telling me 'you're pretty but just not my type.'" She rolls her eyes while curling her fingers into air quotes.

My brain stalls like a car with a bad clutch on a San Francisco hill. It makes no sense that no one is falling into a lust induced fog when close to her, while I'm constantly losing the battle to get my head out of the clouds.

"I just don't want you to start whatever this is going to be and think I'll have something to add because I don't. I'm practically brand new and have nothing to offer you in return."

Practically brand new shouldn't have my knees weakening but I grip the counter for support anyway. Isn't my number one rule no virgins? Apparently Harper being on the cusp is enough for me to catapult that rule out like it never existed.

I circle the island to get to her. The barstool screeches against the floor as I pull her chair so she's facing me. "I wouldn't care if you came here and everything in the folder is marked off as an item you've done, what matters to me is you're here."

Her breath cascades out. "Okay," she whispers.

"Do you have anything to say about my original statement?"

I didn't realize how bad I want to know if she watches the way I watch her.

Her tongue darts out and I fight the urge to press my mouth against hers. Timidly, she replies, "I like knowing that you've been watching me."

"Oh, my Sweet Girl, you have no idea." I turn the chair so she's facing the island again. "Finish eating and then we'll go over exactly what you're looking for."

Harper takes another bite without any further prompting and my gut tells me something I already knew; she is going to be perfect.

"Do I get to see your list?" Harper asks, thumbing the edge of the folder in front of her.

"Of course. I'm not here to hide anything from you." Loose paper glides across the table into her waiting hand. She looks it over, too fast to register anything, before setting it back down.

"Harper." Her name comes out as a soft demand. When her eyes lift and meet mine, trepidation fills her rich irises.

"You can ask me anything. Nothing is too small or off limits."

The delicate skin along her throat bobs as she goes back to not looking at me. "Our first time together you were very...um, direct."

"Is that something you didn't like?"

Her hands wave wildly, batting away my question. "No, no, I like it. I was just wondering if there's a name for it."

A soft chuckle slips out and a rose wave colors her cheeks again. "Out of everything you see on the list, your only question is if there's a name for how I act in the bedroom?"

"Kinda." She shrugs, looking between me and the list. "And to know whatever 'cock warming' is."

My next laugh comes out as a bark. "God, you're going to be so fun."

The way she looks at me stirs my darker desires, the ones that want to own her completely. Steal her away from the world and selfishly keep her to myself. There's nothing wrong with what I like, crave, even. It hurts no one, doesn't break any laws, and yet it's an aspect of my life I'm forced to keep deep in the shadows. Not that I'm trying to showcase it but there's always a chance of ridicule. Which is why I don't date, and my metaphorical punch card to Midnights is overloaded.

"Labels don't mean much to me but if you want a name for it, I'd say I fall somewhere between a soft dom or plea-sure dom."

A small noise of acknowledgment comes from Harper's side of the table.

"Do you know what either of those are?"

"Not really."

"Look at my list and tell me what you see." Her eyes dart back down, and she flicks through the pages, but a bit slower this time.

Ultimately she shrugs. "A lot of things marked as inter-ested."

"What's not marked as interested?"

Harper lifts the paper and skims through again. I wait before feeding her the answer.

"No blood or impact play, no harsh degradation. No spanking even. I don't want to cause or see you in any pain. That's not what this is about, all I want is your pleasure. Everything that is marked are aspects that I engage in be-cause I know they will bring you the most out of body experience. That's all I want."

There's a slight shift in her. Her hips rock in the chair across from me as her neck cranes side to side before she sets the paper back down. "So you like giving?"

"More than you know," I say and relish in the way her face flushes. "Can I show you?"

Her hands fall into her lap. Everything goes still. Seconds drag on for eons until finally she nods.

"Come here, Harper." I request, wearing the heavy air of authority like a comforting mask. I like to be the one to call the shots, I like to give orders. But what I love most of all is the precise moment when control is relinquished and placed entirely onto me. Giving me the power to do whatever I want. And as Harper slowly stands without any further command and walks over to me all I want is to pull every ounce of pleasure I can from her body.

Today couldn't have been better, the outfit she has on is one of my favorites. Honestly, anytime Harper is in a skirt is my favorite and right now is no different as my cock stiffens in my pants.

"I like being in control. At work, in my personal life, in the bedroom," I start saying as I lean forward, placing both hands on her hips and guiding her so she's in between my knees and her back is to the table. "But I don't get off on controlling by fear or punishment or pain."

Harper watches with rapt attention as I grip her hips, lifting her to sit on the table. Fingers melt into the softness of her. The fabric of her skirt flows like water as I guide the soft material up her legs. I want at least ten more in her closet.

"I prefer a more gentle approach. Coaxing you into submission rather than demanding it from you."

Fabric pools around her waist and onto the table. Harper leans back on her hands with a few labored breaths moving her entire chest.

"Does that make sense, Sweet Girl?" Harper opens up beautifully when I spread my legs with her feet pressing into my knees. There's not an inch of skin I don't want to see, but having her partially clothed, with her most intimate space on display for me, is the type of torture I'd die to experience.

"Yes," she answers, a breathy whisper of a word.

"I also get enjoyment out of how many times I can make you come and all the different ways I can get you there. Probably even more than finishing myself, if I'm honest."

"Really?" It's not the first I've heard the questioning tone when I make that confession, but at the very least, this will be the last.

"Really."

All I see are pale pink cotton panties and momentarily I'm rendered mute. Nearly non-existent and molded to her center. Nothing to hide the fact she's turned on and has probably been since she got here as a small damp spot blooms in the middle.

I'm fixated, salivating and trying my fucking hardest not to dive face first into nirvana. "I want you to remember you can stop all of this or even some of it at any time. I may be in control but you have all the power."

Our eyes meet. Ice to earth. Matching unbridled heat swimming through our connection. "I don't want to stop," she says, and it's exactly what I've been waiting for.

Reaching forward and hooking my fingers under the band, I peel her underwear from her body slowly, and then unconsciously pocket them. My knees slide out further to spread her wider, before giving her first order. "Show me what makes you feel good."

Her eyebrows knit together, pouty lips parting with an unspoken question. "Don't tell me you've spent all these years neglecting this pretty pussy too." I run the back of my finger along her center, forcing a sharp breath into her chest. I do it again for good measure.

"Show me how you like to be touched."

Her lip is in a vice-like grip between her teeth but slowly she reaches down, only hesitating for a second before doing exactly what I asked.

Inside every molecule in my body takes flight at the sight of her pink, wet center and I have to press my palm against my zipper for even the smallest amount of relief.

Harper knows exactly what she needs. Each movement is executed with calculated precision. Years of being the only one to bring herself over the edge. Burgundy painted fingertips tread slowly through the dark thatch of hair covering the top of her mound, the rest is bare and slick with arousal.

Chain me to the chair because I don't know how else to keep myself from sliding into her in the next five seconds. One look at her like this, spread wide for me, her wall of inhibitions slowly crumbling as she spins tight circles around her clit and it makes my cock weep.

Harper's head falls back. A breathy moan falling from her lips

"You're beautiful, Harper. I should take a picture of you like this, spread wide and dripping wet. Hang it in my office like the art you keep in yours."

She murmurs something incoherent, circling her fingers tighter, quicker. Chest heaving and hips lifting, she's seconds from tipping over the edge. "Stop." I instruct.

Harper's hand stills, head lifts, and with eyes wild, looks at me with a pained expression. "What happened? Did I do something wrong?"

"Of course not. Touch yourself again," I say, reassuring and tender.

She wants to ask a thousand questions, I can see each of them brewing behind her eyes. A precious sort of agony circles her irises but she complies. The edge comes a bit quicker. I wait until her head drops back onto the table and I tell her to stop again.

Harper's a natural, even if she stops with a heavy groan. Relinquishing control isn't easy, it goes against everything we're ever taught. Humans are wired to make decisions, thousands of them every day. When to wake up, what to wear, what errands need to be done. We're overrun by lists, appointments to remember, and jobs where we juggle endless tasks. We go to bed then do it all over again, day after day. Shutting our brains off in order for someone else to make the decisions, is an intimate act, even more so when it's for someone to tell you when to come.

"Start again."

"Nolan, I don't understand."

"You marked edging off on the list, this is your first lesson. Do you want to keep going?"

She lifts up on her elbows and stares at me. Each of us breathing heavily in tandem. "Yes," she finally replies.

"Yes, what, Sweet Girl?"

There's a pause. Any answer would work, there's nothing in particular in mind but I'm curious about what will come out of her mouth.

"Yes, Sir." It's a timid answer, probably foreign as it rolls off her tongue but God dammit if it's not the sweetest syllable.

Fuck.

Fuck, fuck, fuck.

CHAPTER ELEVEN

FEBRUARY 5

It slips out without resistance. *Sir.* I'm not sure if he was actually looking for me to call him anything specific or anything at all. I don't really know what to think. I'm not even sure if I am thinking at this point but I know this is everything I was missing.

"Again," Nolan says.

Maybe I'm not cut out for this, time has barely ticked by since I laid back on the table and yet an eternity appears to have lapsed. "Nolan, I don't know—"

"If you need to stop, use your safe word." He waits, sitting in his chair like it's a throne. Nolan holds my gaze. Where my eyes are pleading, his are determined and with that, I fall deeper into my own lust.

I don't move and I don't want to use the word. I want to come. I want his hands on me. I want him. I want a thousand things all at the same time, things I didn't even know were possible to want.

My fingers find my clit again, swollen and aching. I've done this countless times, under the cover of darkness in my own room and never in front of anyone. Each breath is sharper than the last, each swirl shoots electricity through my soul. My toes curl and I know I'm seconds away from tumbling blindly into euphoria. "Please," I breathe into the quiet house.

Finally Nolan's hands are on me, roaming up my legs, spreading me wider, right to the edge of pain but I'm still blissfully drowning in technicolor pleasure. Bright, swirling hues bloom behind my lids and I'm breathing in colors I've never seen before. "You're beautiful, Harper. The type of woman men crawl across deserts for. The type of woman men start wars over. My type of woman," his voice thick with unmistakable devotion. When he stands, the metal from his belt clinks and the soft undeniable sound of his zipper lowering fills my ears like a symphony. Nolan settles between my legs, and as if this is our daily routine, my legs find their home around his waist.

"Stop."

I whine but follow his order.

"You've done so well, but I need to be inside of you. I have to feel you or I might go mad." I can feel him notch the tip of his cock at my entrance.

Fire blazes along my skin, dancing across my chest and down my stomach, settling deep in my core I feel alive. "Please, Nolan. Please, plea—" I beg with a sobbing breath that fractures on the last word.

He swipes himself through the obscene wetness coating my center and dripping down my thighs. I need him. I need him like air. I need him like religion, a singular deity to hang all my hopes and dreams on.

My eyes crack open enough to watch as he enters me. One swiftly, until his entire length is inside of me, I force my eyes to stay open and revel in the bliss overcoming his features.

"I could live here," he says to the ceiling, slowly dragging his cock out before pushing it back in. "Inside of you is better than any heaven I'll end up in."

Nolan replaces my fingers with his own. He swipes his thumb once across me and I nearly explode.

Twice.

Three agonizingly slow passes before he drags his length out of me again and slides back in. Nolan drags my finishing line further and further away. He snaps into me with a relentless pace, before stalling and going back to thumbing my clit. Keeping this patterning until I'm a mess of nearly incoherent noises.

The dining room fills with the sound of my throaty pleas and flesh striking flesh. I'm moments away from losing reality when his voice breaks through. "Come for me, Harper."

I detonate and long awaited relief sweeps through my veins.

Without realizing it, I was waiting for his instructions. My back bows off the table, eyes squeezed shut as stars erupt like a firework finale. My fingers curl around his wrist where he's keeping my thighs spread open and fucks me through my orgasm.

I'm boneless and floating, riding on the final waves as Nolan finishes, spilling into me with stuttering hips and a guttural, almost vulgar groan.

Between panting breaths and sweat soaked skin a connection fuses between us. Welding a bond

Nolan pulls out from me, eyes once again glued to my thighs and where his cum slowly starts to pool onto the dining table.

"God, you're perfect."

I can get used to this.

For Wednesday, my task list is entirely too long, but I have to push most of it aside, and I'm heading over to the only hotel in Cupid, where the gala will take place. Honestly, I'm not sure how to be productive after last night.

I'm halfway out of my office when Nolan appears in the doorway.

There should be a rule put into place saying Nolan can't walk out of the house looking like sin incarnate before noon. Eros, an aptly given name. He strides into my office, and swings the door shut behind him, forcing me to step backward. "Where are you off to?"

"Venue check, I want to get over there before lunch." He takes a couple more steps toward me. "Why?"

He examines me, slowly dragging his gaze from the tips of my toes back up until he meets my eyes. "Come over tonight." Not a question, not really a demand either, but my stomach drops at his words regardless.

"Again?" For some reason when we agreed to this arrangement, I thought maybe we'd get together a few times here and there, most likely on a weekend. What I didn't expect is the want sparking in his eyes mid morning on a work day.

"Yes, again. Tomorrow, too."

I laugh as a response. "You're joking."

An atmospheric change occurs in my small government office. Air still, the temperature rockets making my sweater unbearably warm as he pulls to his full height, towering over me without making me feel caged in. "I wasn't joking, Harper, I don't think I can function properly if I don't get a taste of you every—"

He takes another step toward me.

"Single."

Another step.

"Day."

I have half a mind to fall back on my desk and give him exactly what he wants. But the door opens before I can lean back.

"Harper—" Sadie's pitchy voice cuts through the veil. Nolan takes a small step back. I feel like I'm about to have a heart attack from the sudden switch. Sadie's gaze bounces between the limited space between Nolan and I. "Am I interrupting something?"

We speak at the same time but not with the same answer. Our mixup has Sadie's eyebrow skyrocketing and eyes doubling in size.

Flicking my gaze over to Nolan, I convey some sort of 'what the hell' look before answering. "No, Sadie, you're not."

But Nolan just can't keep his mouth shut. "I was just asking Harper if she needed any help with the upcoming ball."

Sadie perks up, entering further into the room with quick steps. "Of course," she says with a new lightness in her voice. One that's entirely fake and reserved for Nolan. Anyone with eyes around the building knows she's been trying to land her claws in him since day one. "Please let me know if I can be of any help, Harper. I love throwing parties."

Rocking back on my heels, I look between the two of them. "Yeah, this is a little more than throwing a party." It's impossible to keep the disdain out of my voice.

Her eyes narrow, lips curling into a slight sneer before vanishing in the blink of an eye. "Well, you know where to find me. I'm always happy to help." She turns and leaves, apparently forgetting whatever it is she came in here for in the first place.

"Want me to fire her?" Nolan sneaks up behind me to say.

"What? No." I pause for a moment after the word. "No, she just needs to stay far away from the planning."

The movement is minuscule, but from the corner of my eye, Nolan's hand drifts up, and brushes through the hair at the end of my ponytail. Twirling the strands around his fingers. "All you have to do is ask," he states with a voice like it belongs in the clouds.

"So what, all I have to do is say the word and she'll be gone?"

"All you have to do is ask, and I'll give you anything you want."

When I turn, my hair pulls from his grasp but brings us face to face. Being this close to him envelopes me into his gravity, pulling at something deep inside my chest until it teases the surface. I'm not stupid enough to think this can be something that lasts, I'm not even quite sure if that's something I want but the desire flowing between us is more than a surface level feeling. That much I do know.

"So, tonight then?" I say as his icy blue eyes bounce around my features.

Shoving his hands into his pockets, he takes a step back as a smile breaks across his face. "Tonight."

CHAPTER TWELVE

FEBRUARY 6

THREE NIGHTS IN A ROW— too much and not enough time together. If I could, I would spend every night in Nolan's bed. But unfortunately for me, I actually have to get some work done.

"I can't see you tonight," I say for the fifth time, hating myself a little bit more for it.

City Hall has been empty for hours, and with no one around to catch us, I've perched myself on Nolan's lap, and have been reluctant to move since. Not that he's making it easy.

He's buried his face in the crook of my shoulder, nuzzling the soft skin which muffles his words. "And remind me again why?"

"Because I have things to do, Nolan. Things I should have been home two hours ago to start." It's a half truth, but he didn't need to know that. I would be happy to drive back out to his house again, like I did last night and the night before and when he first asked. The word 'yes' jumped in my throat, practically begging to be said.

It's been three days. Three of them, that's it, and I can feel the threads beginning to stitch together, binding myself to him in a way that I should not be feeling. Space would do us both some good, and on a personal note, my vagina some good. Going from no sex to being bent, twisted, pulled, and pushed in every position known to man, and some that weren't, is wreaking havoc on my joints.

And the Cupid Ball is less than two weeks away, and I haven't even begun sewing the table runners I said I was going to make. Plus, I still need to verify the rest of the vendors' arrival times, review the menu proofs the local printer emailed earlier today, and send all the final payments.

Oh, and find a dress, which somehow always ends up being my last task. But I don't even want to start thinking about braving a department store, especially when I know I won't find anything in my size.

Which reminds me. "I still have your credit card from when I had to book the new vendor. Let me go get it before I forget again." I'm not even an inch off his lap before he pulls me back down.

"Hmm-hmm. Keep it, I don't care, I don't want you out of this position."

"I can't keep your card, Nolan. Just let me get it for you."

I'm shackled into place again. "And I said no." His voice takes on the tone I now associate with his *other side.* This is a command, one I want to follow. "Do you want another lesson?" His question is soft as velvet, caressing the side of my neck, as his lips press against my pulse.

"Depends."

A disappointing tsk comes from behind me. "It's a yes or no, Harper."

Not a single cell in my body wants to say no. "Yes, Sir."

Lucky for him, the morning version of myself slipped on a long flowing skirt.

Nolan's hands skate carelessly slow up my thighs, under my skirt and to my hips. I keep waiting for the moment where his touch doesn't ignite a response in me, but it hasn't happened yet. "If I remember correctly, and I am, your words a few days ago were 'to know whatever cock warming is'." He makes quick work of my underwear while he speaks, slipping his hands up my skirt, peeling them from my body and pocketing my underwear again before I have a chance to take my next breath. "I have a few emails I need to send and I would very much like it if you sat right here while I worked."

This seems a lot tamer than what I imagined. "I just sit on your lap without underwear?" I question because that can't possibly be right.

"Oh, no, my Sweet Girl." His voice is low against the shell of my ear as he snakes one arm around my waist, lifting my body like I'm nothing.

"What are you—*oh*—" My last word is a gasp. In the span of a millisecond, I've gone from empty to overly full. My breath, my thoughts, my sense of up and down disappears, and behind my eyes, a blinding light takes over.

Turns out it's not simply sitting on his lap with no underwear. I'm impaled on Nolan's cock. My eyes grow two sizes at the sudden intrusion, and my heart leaps from its normal resting spot in my chest and lodges itself into my throat.

Nolan strokes his hands down the length of my back, sending shivers over every inch of skin. "Now I need you to be very still. If you move, then I won't be able to type, and the longer we'll have to stay just like this." He smooths my skirt back down, arranging it so if someone were to see it would simply look like I'm simply sitting on his lap. "Can you do that for me?"

My brain can't compute whatever it is he's asking. The only thing it can come up with is the word 'full'. I feel so incredibly and gloriously full. It's unlike anything else I've felt and has emotions I don't even have names for flickering to life.

Nolan reaches around me, pulling his keyboard closer and it finally registers he's not lying. He's going to start working again but I don't want that. There's no possible way I can sit still with him inside me. Not when every nerve ending throughout my body flares to life, demanding something happen.

Anything at this point would do and it hasn't even been a full minute. I know, I've been watching the clock. Slowly, I roll my hips backward, searching for anything to ease the tension that is slowly circling my insides.

"Harper," he warns, "no moving."

A whimper pushes past my lips. "You can't seriously expect me to sit here with you inside of me."

"I can, and I do." He begins plucking away at his keyboard.

"But—"

"No buts. Sit still, or we'll be here all night."

He must have an extreme amount of confidence in his stamina.

"I just," I start with a whine. I'm not going to make it to whatever time limit he's set in his head. The urge to fuck myself on him fells like I'm being dragged under relentless ocean waves. "I can do all the work, please, Sir."

His fingers still, even his breath stalls. An eerie silence falls over us. Only my rapid pants of wantonness fill his office before he starts typing again but it's short lived.

Nolan leans back in his chair. A deep moan reverberates in my chest.

"How was your day?" he asks nonchalantly. As if we're friends catching up over coffee.

"You're not seriously trying to make small talk with me right now, are you?"

"What, are you busy?" The smile in his voice is deafening. I don't even have to look at him to know it's there.

His hands drift from the keyboard, work already forgotten. Or perhaps this was the plan all along - sit me on his lap and watch me descend into a thick fog, straddling the fine line between pain and pleasure. I'm so unbelievably full that my ability to string a sentence together is quickly fading.

"Harper," he says, cutting through the haze. "Is this okay?" There's a tenderness in his voice I've grown to crave. I want to answer him, tell him yes, that in fact I'm perfectly content as I ascend to a plane of existence most people never reach.

Deep in the pit of my stomach, pressure brews, threatening an explosion that would level this building. Each time I think I have an answer for him, the words dissolve like sugar in water, leaving only the feel of hands on my thighs and the ever large presence of him inside of me the only things worth focusing on.

I manage a weak response. "It's good. I'm good."

Nothing eloquent floats through my mind, only soft nothingness, but the shudder in his chest makes me think he understands.

Soft hands run up the length of my arms, smoothing the goosebumps pricking my skin. "I didn't see you much today." He sounds remorseful, hesitant even. Almost as if those few words hold more meaning than he's letting on.

But the small talk might actually kill me.

I swallow. "I had a school tour come through, took up most of my day."

Nolan hums, his hand still roaming across my body.

"What's your favorite color?"

"Oh my God, you are trying to kill me. Didn't you say you had work to do?"

"I do, but this is a lot more fun."

I peek over my shoulder. "What? Torturing me?"

"You know what to do if you want to stop"

I don't answer.

"Exactly, because you like this, don't you, Sweet Girl? You like being helpless in my lap. You like being full of me, dancing on the edge of oblivion." He suffers again. "Barely any time has passed, but you're so close, aren't you?"

He shifts, forcing fireworks to explode as I squeeze my eyes shut and clamp down on my tongue to keep from crying out.

"You don't have to be quiet. In fact, I prefer you loud."

"Do you know why I like this?" he asks.

I shake my head, falling forward onto my elbows. The sudden change in position pushes him further into me, forcing a groan from my chest.

"Because it's a way for you to let go and give yourself over to me. It's not overtly stimulating, it's a way for you to be in the moment, with me, here. A way for us to be connected, and I like being able to do that for you."

With his finger, a feather light line drags down my spine, spiking of debilitating pleasure to bloom under my skin. My body shivers. "How long do I have to wait?"

His body vibrates with a low hum as he contemplates. Whatever answer he gives, I'll happily take it, because at this point I can't tell if I want to stay like this, skating along the brink of exhilaration, or if I want to jump from his lap, lay face down on his desk, and beg for him to fuck me.

"I'll let you know when your time is up."

What an agonizingly beautiful response.

—-

Fifteen glorious, torturous minutes later, he pushes his keyboard back, closes out all his windows, and shuts off his computer. Whatever comes next is sure to be mind blowing but instead of any sort of movement, he asks me a question. "Do you have a dress to wear to the ball yet?"

I don't move, not until he tells me, but I answer, even with fading thoughts swirling down a drain, unlikely to come back. "What?"

"A dress, have you gone out to buy one yet?"

"No."

"Good, tomorrow we'll go and get you one."

It doesn't seem worth it to fight the offer and I need to get one anyway. "Thank you."

I watch him smile from over my shoulder. A soft, tender pull at the corner of his lips. "How do you feel?" he finally asks a few seconds later.

"Good," I answered honestly. "Very full. Very, very aroused. I think even one small move will send me flying into an orgasm."

As he laughs at my last comment, I can't help but think about how much I like hearing it. He's laughing more around me and not only when we're in positions like this. But even during quick interactions at work.

We've tumbled into a peculiar relationship where a whole new side of him, one I never knew existed, is wide open specifically for me. I get his quiet laughs, his longing looks, his hands on my curves, and even though they are all given in secret, I wouldn't change a single thing about what we have.

"How do you feel?" I ask, filling the silence. As much as he says this is all for me, I really like knowing if I'm pleasing him too.

Surprise jumps in his eyes before he answers. "I also feel on edge, like one stroke of this wet, tight pussy will have me spilling into you. And I feel proud, proud and horny."

"Proud?"

"Of you, of course. Placing your pleasure and curiosity into my hands is a gift, seeing you take to it so naturally, and that I'm the one you choose to give it to, all of that makes me feel proud."

All I can manage is a quiet "oh" because out of all the things I assumed he might say, proud wasn't amongst them.

No one's ever told me they were proud of me. Not my friends, not the people I work with and certainly not my family. At some point, I stopped even reaching out to people for the word and decided as long as I am proud of myself, that's all that matters.

I didn't expect hearing the words from someone else's mouth would have tears rushing to the surface.

Nolan shifts forward and my eyes flutter shut, forcing the tears back. I've been patient, and now I get my reward.

CHAPTER THIRTEEN

Nolan

IT'S A SUBLIME VERSION of heaven when I'm inside Harper. A place where happiness seems endless and every moment is better than the last. A place I could live and die in, forgetting the world even existed. And I'm dreading the day all of this has to come to an end. I've fallen faster than light travels across the universe, harder than a meteor impact into Earth. Devastating, world ending, because even though it feels impossible all I want is to keep her.

"You've done so well, Sweet Girl," I murmur with my lips against the soft skin of her shoulder.

Harper lets out a small whimper as I shift my hips. The sound claws up my spine and even though it didn't seem possible, my cock hardens even more inside of her.

"Nolan, please tell me it's time to move. Please tell me it's time. Otherwise I'm going to explode," she laughs between her pleas. She's perfect, she was perfect before we ever started all of this, but discovering the way we seamlessly fit together has only solidified my opinion of how exquisite she truly is.

Gently gripping her hips, I lift Harper off my lap. She follows my lead with a tiny whimper, leaving my dick shiny with her arousal. When her hands hit my desk, hunger strikes low in my stomach.

My slacks are ruined.

Harper's been a dripping mess since I sat her on my lap. A shudder wracks through my body at the thought. "You did so good," I praise, dancing my hand along each vertebra, pushing gently once my palm is flat between her shoulder blades. Pressing her chest into the oak grain.

My hand slips down, between her slick thighs, and her words drift off. She's so fucking wet but I want her messier.

I want her scrambling for her next breath and dripping onto the floor. I want to watch her melt into a puddle of pleasure, one she'll grow to associate with me, that keeps her coming back for more. Day after day after day.

"Nolan, I need—"

Pressing two fingers inside, I'm enveloped in a heat I hope I never get used to. Harper's fingers claw at the desk at the intrusion before she squeezes her dark lust blown eyes shut and expels an explosive breath. "I know, Sweet Girl. This cunt is a needy little thing, isn't it?"

She nods with her cheek stuck to the desk. I drag my hand back and plunge back inside.

Harper whimpers.

"That's my Sweet Girl. Can you take one more?" I wait and only once she nods, I add another finger.

My skin pricks with satisfaction over how well she adapts. I go back to slowly thrusting in and out of her. Harper writhes beneath me, soft, needy whimpers falling from her lips until she eventually begins rocking her hips, fucking herself on my fingers. When her cunt flutters around me, I know she's close.

Pulling from her, I step back.

"No, what? Where are you going?" Harper glances over her shoulder, brows pinching and glossy eyed.

"Spread yourself for me, show me how wet you are."

135

Without hesitation, both of Harper's hands lift, and grip onto each plump cheek. Dark red nails dig into the flesh, pulling herself open wide without shame. Pride swells in my chest with how fast she's taken to our dynamic, not a hint of shame or embarrassment. None of the timidness from the first night. In its place, a truer version of herself emerges. Full of confidence and it's only been days.

She's bloomed into a woman I never want to be without.

It makes me want things I never allowed myself to feel before. Makes me want to know what she'll be like in a few months or years. Would she allow her confidence in the bedroom to melt into her daily life? Use her newly uncovered faith in herself to get what she wants? Harper's meant for bigger things than what Cupid has to offer and I... I want to be a part of it.

And that thought alone kills me.

My fist circles my aching shaft, pumping it once as I step toward her. Harper continues to look up at me from over her shoulder. A dreamy smile on her face as I notch myself at her entrance. With one swift movement as I enter her completely, and without resistance, groaning each other's names simultaneously.

For a moment, I'm rendered speechless, immobile even, while I'm bombarded by a million zaps of electricity over my skin, my blood replaced by fireworks. I bend forward, brushing my lips against her spine before pulling out and snapping back in.

The room fills with the sound of our skin and Harper's cries of bliss. And everything else in the world fades away. The sky could come crashing down, or the Earth could split under the sole of my shoes, but I wouldn't notice or care. This moment with Harper is the only thing I care about.

"I could do this forever. A life with this pussy, this ass...you." Dizziness takes over my senses, leaving me feeling drunk. "I could keep you forever. You, with your humor and compassion, everything about you drives me fucking wild and I don't want it to stop." Words pour out of me, ones that have no business being uttered and should stay locked in the dark corner of my mind, but when I'm around Harper, I can't help myself. She's an elixir I want coursing through my veins for the rest of eternity, no matter the cost.

Heavy, shaky breaths are the only sound I get from her but that's okay. I'll tell her again, I'll tell her every day if I have to because at this moment, I've done the quickest one eighty, deciding: I *am* keeping her. I don't know how but I'll figure that out later.

"Oh, God." Harper gasps, nearly choking on the words as each thrust comes faster than the last. My hands continue to dig into her hips and my only hope is that she'll walk around the next few days with my marks on her.

"Fall for me, Harper." I pull out, only to drive back inside of her. "You know what I want and I know you want to give it to me."

I'm staring down the barrel of my own orgasm as it spirals up my spine. But I need hers first, I will always need hers first.

Another minute and she breaks beautifully, coming as she cries out my name. I follow her almost immediately, spilling into her until my hips stutter and my lungs strain for air.

My head drops back. Our breaths even out, my heart stops hammering inside my chest and something creaks from outside my office but I can only stare at the ceiling as I float back down from heaven.

"Do you want to see?" Harper's voice cracks through the haze.

I look down in time to see her place a hand on each cheek again and pull herself apart. A mixture of us drips from her entrance.

All I can muster is a deep sigh in response. How many times can I call this woman perfect before it starts to lose its luster? I am going to take a guess and say the number probably doesn't exist.

CHAPTER FOURTEEN

FEBRUARY 7

GOD FORBID A MAN like Nolan Archer shop at the mall for clothes. No, too much beneath a man of his stature. Instead we're two hours away from Cupid at some boutique with a name I can't pronounce where the clothes don't even have price tags. The store drips in white linen and gold baroque accents, doing its best to trick you into thinking you've been transported to Paris.

Saleswomen flock to Nolan the moment we step through the door. They fawn over him and if this place didn't also carry men's clothing, I would be spiraling thinking I'm just one of many women he's brought here. But in a shocking turn of events, they didn't even blink when Nolan told them we're here for me and not him.

All at once they swarm me, guiding me to the back dressing rooms where measuring tapes are being placed in every crevice and along every limb, around my waist and falling from my hips. And then they're gone so quickly my head spins.

"Wow," I say, my voice loaded with shock. I glance over at Nolan, leaning against the wall opposite of the dressing room now overflowing with tulle, satin and organza. I'm having trouble believing all this is even happening. The sex was already hard enough to believe but us together, in the day, running errands, is a fantasy I don't even let myself have.

"What?"

"Nothing, I just didn't expect all of...this. I'm used to the mall experience, you know perusing racks of dresses, trying them on myself in front of a mirror, and then stopping by Cinnabon after my inevitable breakdown when nothing fits."

Nolan pushes off the wall and steps closer to me. "Is it too much?" he asks, dragging a finger down the exposed skin of my arm.

"No, just different."

In a moment so domestic and so intimate that makes my cheeks burn, he leans down and brushes his lips against my shoulder. "Good. You deserve expensive things, Harper, and I like being the one to give them to you."

My heartbeat stalls.

"I don't need things from you, Nolan," I say the words with blistering honesty. "I just like being with you."

The world doesn't halt at my confession, nothing falls from the sky and the ground doesn't crack beneath us but a look passes over his face. So devastatingly tender, my throat begins to burn.

The spell between us breaks when the saleswoman comes back with a final dress. "Mrs. Archer, we're ready for you." With how fast they moved when we got here, they must not have realized I wasn't his wife.

My mouth opens to correct them, but Nolan leans in, presses a chaise kiss against my cheek and says, "Make sure you come out and show me each one, Mrs. Archer."

I like the way that sounds. Way too much.

·♥·♥·♥·♥·♥·

The first four dresses are awful. One doesn't zip, and the other, I can't even get up past my hips. One I don't even bother trying on and another my boobs didn't fit in, and not in the fun sexy way. The room was closing in on me, growing into a furnace with every passing second. What was I thinking, I should have known a high-end boutique carries only sample sizes. As if trying on clothes isn't hard enough for me most days, this was the start of a nightmare.

I'm tumbling head first into a panic attack when the door clicks open and Nolan slips inside.

"What are you doing? You can't be in here," I whisper as he shuts the door and clicks the lock into place.

"Says who?"

"Uhh, common society?"

He rolls his eyes. "You haven't come out to show me any of them."

I instinctively cross my arms over my chest, as if that will keep my insecurity from pouring out onto the floor between us. "Yeah, well, none of them fit. Can't really walk out of here if the top doesn't cover my nipples."

He glances down at my chest.

"Not this one," I swat his shoulder. "This one's fine."

More like it was the first one to fit. It's a stunning deep burgundy, floor-length gown with delicate flower beads in the same color that sparkle with every move. It doesn't look terrible, like I convinced myself it would when I slipped into it, but dress shopping is never a straightforward task. And dress shopping in a place like this, where I'm surprised even one dress fits, makes everything feel like the walls are closing in on me.

"This one is very pretty," he says freely.

I want to agree with him but that spiraling feeling was still coursing through me.

"Are you okay?"

Looking up, I manage a small smile and nod. He doesn't buy it. Not even for a second.

"If this isn't the dress, then we can try another store. We can have one custom made if you want. It doesn't matter, you're beautiful no matter what clothes cover your body."

A burning sensation tears through my chest and it doesn't stop. Not when he pulls me in. Not when he presses his lips against mine, and not when he walks me backward until my back hits the mirror and his thickening length presses against me. The burning morphs into a white hot need for more.

"Do you want another lesson?" he breathes against my lips.

I nod feverously.

Nolan spins me, pressing my ass against his front, turning me toward the mirror. "I was thinking exhibitionism." He drags his hands down the sides of my body. "How does that sound?"

The urge to melt into him pulls at my insides and only deepens as he works open-mouth kisses from my shoulder to my neck. Each one stamping a further claim on me. I can't even grasp a negative word when he starts gathering the thin silk fabric in his hands, dragging it up, exposing my ankles, and then knees, and groans when he realizes I had left my underwear off.

Every touch sends me further away, I'm only faintly aware of the saleswomen talking right outside of the dressing room.

"Nolan," I try to warn, but it comes out as a needy moan when he cups my entire sex with his palm. There isn't nearly enough pressure, but his other hand sits like a vice around my hip, keeping me from seeking out any friction.

"Can you be quiet for me?" He slips a finger through as I fervently nod. "So wet already, what a good girl you are."

This dressing room is not made for two people. With one wall being an entire mirror it feels even smaller but as I stare at his reflection as he works a finger in and out of me I barely even notice. My eyelids fall in heavy blinks as the dress strains around my chest, with each breath.

"Don't want another?"

I want anything he'll give me. And it's a scary sentiment to even think but one that rings true anytime I get around him.

A breathy 'please' manages to escape my mouth without me making the decision. As he works a second finger into me, my next breath catches, stalls, and a deep, chest rattling moan follows it.

"Mrs. Archer, I've left another dress out here I think you'll love."

My eyes fly open. "I—"

He pulls his hand from me and clasps it over my mouth. "Sh, sh, sh, didn't I say you need to be quiet?"

I nod against his hand; my eyes lock with his in the mirror, and without missing a beat, he slides the two fingers between my lips. The taste of myself fills my senses as he eases them back out.

"Mrs. Archer, did you hear me?"

"Answer her," he whispers.

I swallow. "O-okay, thank you," I say, barely able to keep my voice steady.

"You're welcome." Her clicking heels fade down the hallway.

Exhibitionism was on my list as interested, but I didn't really understand it. The thought of people actually watching me didn't really seem appealing but this—this sensation of being consumed by a man who wants to watch me fall apart in public and the fact that someone might hear, or know... I'm definitely into.

"I need you, Sweet Girl, will you be good and take all of me?" His voice strains to keep his composure.

Nolan waits for my nod and before pulling the hem of the dress up past my waist. Threads tear as he bends me forward. "Nolan, the dress," I hiss.

He pushes the head of his cock in, in one fluid motion. "I don't care about the fucking dress." He pulls out and thrusts back in. "We'll buy it and then find you one you really want to wear. I'll buy you a thousand dresses or a whole fucking store." Fingers dig into the soft skin around my hips as he guides my body, sliding back into me.

"Fuck, you feel so good."

Apparently the quiet rule is only for me.

My mouth may not be making a sound but I was certainly making noise. The wet sounds of my arousal fill the room. I'm too far gone to think about any repercussions of this terribly, fantastic decision.

Each thrust of his hips is rough, our reflection in the mirror is obscene. It's dirty. Erotic. It's like being consumed by a rogue ocean wave, tumbling through the water, gasping for breath and not knowing when you will meet the surface again. Terrifying and exhilarating. And possibly the most free I've ever felt.

My climax washes over me quickly and surprises me. "That's my girl, you like that people might hear you fucking your husband, don't you?"

I'm not sure even he knows what he's saying at this point as he loses himself in the moment. The most erotic part about this entire thing isn't fucking in public, or the filth that spills from his mouth, it's the way euphoria seems to take over his perfect features. And the fact that I'm the one responsible for it.

Nolan chases his own climax, spilling into me, and stifling his own sounds of pleasure with his fist between his teeth.

It's quiet as he pulls me upright. If I didn't know any better, I'd think I've downed four shots and then tried to stand up. My knees shake, my head is hazy and heavy, but I am so blissfully happy that I almost forget where we are.

Nolan lets go of the gown, letting it fall to the floor and works the straps over my shoulders before looking at me through the mirror. "This one is very beautiful." His tone, full of warmth, like stepping out into the summer heat.

Blistering and comforting as it envelopes you, promising better days.

"Should I get it?"

"Only if it's the one *you* want, Harper."

I duck my head. "But I want you to like it too," I whisper.

His arms snake around my waist, pulling me in closer and resting his chin in the soft dip between my shoulder and neck. Tiny pricks of his beard in my skin cause me to shudder with a laugh.

He squeezes me tighter. "I like you no matter what you have on."

Our eyes catch in the mirror, we're so different. At first glance, we're pieces belonging to two different puzzles. Nolan's six inches taller than me, and even fully clothed, you'd still know he doesn't have an ounce of fat on his body. Whereas my body completely conceals his as I stand in front of him. My hips wider than I'd like, and my chest always the biggest in the room. Our hair is similar but his is streaked with grey. His blue eyes are like rouge glaciers that were never meant to meet the vast mountains of my own dull brown eyes. We don't look like we belong, but as I study us, there's nothing that has ever seemed more right or more natural.

Even in this clandestine fitting room, with his cum slowly dripping down my thighs, my soul lights up.

I don't want this to ever end. If only I could keep him.

Chapter Fifteen

February 9

"He has a meeting in fifteen minutes, Harper, you can come back," Sadie's borrowed tone of authority snaps. I stop mid step in front of Nolan's office, turn and look at her, wondering what sort of Twilight Zone I stepped into. Since when did Sadie care if anyone was in his office prior to a meeting? When did Sadie start remembering Nolan even had meetings?

"I think it will be just fine, I only need his signature on some expense reports."

Sadie's eyes narrow in a one sided challenge. "You can just give the papers to me and I'll have him sign them after." She sticks her hand out without bothering to stand up from her desk. Perfect french manicured fingers wiggle mid air as if I'm going to walk over and hand them off to her. I've definitely stepped into an alternate universe.

I bite back a laugh at the audacity. "No, thanks."

My hand curls around the door knob when she speaks back up. "Don't think I haven't noticed what you've been doing," she boasts.

My body freezes, ice trickling from the top of my head and cascading down my body.

Sadie is dim at best, but mostly, she's just a nuisance. Malicious was new and unsettling.

What the hell was that supposed to mean? Sadie and I aren't friends, I would barely call her an acquaintance. She's Nolan's secretary of the month, and they're switched out so often sometimes I don't even bother learning their names, but I have nothing against Sadie.

There's no reason for the sudden frigidness filling the room.

And I know she doesn't know about Nolan and I. Nobody does, we've kept it that way on purpose.

I pivot to face her. "Did I do something?"

"If you think you can just change up your outfits, play up your make up a bit more and think he'll notice you, you're wrong."

Nervous laughter bubbles in my throat. "I'm sorry, but now I'm really confused."

"Not like he would look twice at you anyway."

Thick skin is something I developed early in life and this sudden outburst does nothing but bounce right off of me. Sadie's a mean girl, but as simple as a garden cat.

"I don't know what you're talking about but maybe you should spend more time doing your job correctly than worrying about what I'm wearing."

She scoffs. "I'm only here because your dad begged my father to let me work here."

"What?"

She shrinks back a bit, realizing she said something she shouldn't have uttered a word about. "Never mind, just know Nolan will never see you. He's used to a certain type of woman and you don't fit." Sadie watches me, waiting for the moment her words draw the blood she is desperate for but it never comes.

Silence sometimes is the loudest thing a person can say, and if I were a slightly better person, I'd just walk away. I can't tell her about Nolan and me, obviously, but something about her comment nudges me into a possessive territory. But I tell her the truth. "And neither are you."

I walk into Nolan's office without waiting for her response, and for good measure, I grin over my shoulder at her as Nolan's voice rings with my name. I keep my eyes locked on Sadie as I shut the door with her still at her desk.

Spinning toward Nolan once the door clicks shut, I let out an exasperated sigh. "You will not believe what Sadie just said to me," I say, dropping into the chair in front of him and placing the reports on his desk.

I really did come here for signatures.

His face drops at the mention of her name. "Please don't tell me, she has been on my last nerve the past couple of days."

At least we're on the same page and it has me hiding a smile.

"Your father invited me to another dinner tonight and I haven't been able to get out of it. I'm sure he's invited Sadie again too."

"Why would he invite Sadie?"

Something is definitely going on, I just don't know what my father wants with Sadie.

Before he can answer, my dad appears as if we conjured the devil himself with the mere mention of his name. And again, he barely notices me.

"Nolan, we're still on for tonight, right?" His booming voice takes over the silence that was passing over us when I asked about Sadie. "And don't give me some bullshit excuse, you already got out of last week's dinner."

"Dan, Harper and I were in the middle of a meeting."

He finally looks over at me, flecks of disdain in the same color eyes I see in the mirror everyday. "Hello, Harper, Nolan and I have a meeting in ten minutes, you know?" he states, like I'm here specifically to inconvenience him. The fact I work in the building and that Nolan is my boss means nothing to him.

"I'm aware." I turn to Nolan and push the folder closer to him. "I just need these signed. Let me know when you're done, I'll come back and get them."

He nods.

I'm halfway from my seat when Nolan speaks. "Are you coming to dinner tonight too, Harper?" My dad's head snaps to Nolan and then to me with a look that lowers the temperature of the room.

Nerves swim in my stomach. "Umm..."

My dad jumps in before I can really answer. "Harper's probably busy with the ball and doesn't have time to join us. That's why your mother never reached out, I'm sure."

Nolan answers for me. "Oh, of course." And then turns back to me again. "But surely you have time for dinner with your parents and their boring old friend right?"

I don't know how I'm supposed to answer this. "I—"

"Great, Dan, you said dinner at seven? We'll see you tonight, Harper, and I'll have these back to you before we leave for the day."

In a perfect world, I would have walked up to my parent's sprawling estate with my head held high. I'd push through the doors without knocking and when they saw me, shock wouldn't be the first thing I witnessed. My brother and sister wouldn't lean into each other, whispering back and forth while stealing glances my way. My mother wouldn't loudly proclaim how inconvenient it was to put out another place setting.

In a perfect world, this house would feel like my home, but it doesn't. Instead, it feels like a tomb I once escaped.

People filled my parents' house, mingling around the rooms, and it was easy enough to lose myself among them

— or at least it was. Then dinner was served, and I found myself sandwiched between Nolan and the mayor from a neighboring town but also in my siblings' line of sight.

"Hi, sorry I'm late." A too fake voice cut through the awkward silence of dinner. Nolan and I turn in time to see Sadie sashay comfortably into my parent's dining room. She leans down, brushing a kiss against my mother's cheek before squealing into my sister's outstretched arms.

Which makes no sense.

Granted, I don't keep up with all my sister's friends, we're not close enough to run in the same circles for me to know who she spends her time with but I should know if my coworker was friends with my sister. Right?

Sadie slides into the chair next to Hallie, pulls the linen napkin from its silver ring, and delicately places it in her lap. Predatory eyes scan the table with eagerness until she finds exactly who she's here for.

My father is as subtle as a cactus in a snow field. It's no secret he's used the secretary position as a personal match-making service for Nolan. Every candidate that's graced that chair is a carbon copy of the one before, but I can't figure out why he is so bent on putting Sadie in Nolan's crosshairs. What is it about her, and why did my dad even care about who his friend dates?

Sadie's sights land on Nolan and a smile crosses her face that makes even my teeth ache. "Nolan, it's nice to see you make it out of the office." Her eyes slide to me. "And Harper's here."

Sadie's face always does this thing when she sees something she doesn't care for. Like anytime an email is sent to her requiring her to do her actual job, women in clothes she deems tacky, carbs, or in this instance, me. Her eyes widen while her features pinch inward, like a lemon has been shoved in her mouth.

Hallie leans over, whispering something that has Sadie throwing her head back, laughing loud enough that the entire table looks over. Which is what she wanted.

"What's so funny down there?" my mother interjects, desperate to be part of my sister's life in any way.

Sadie looks around the long table, making sure everyone's eyes are on her. Which they are, or at least all but one set because when I turn to the side, planning the quickest way out, Nolan's looking back at me. Baby blue and tainted with an echo of concern. Under the table, away from everyone, his fingers skim the side of my thigh.

A haunting reminder that we are a secret.

"Oh, nothing, just Hallie was reminding me of the last Cupid Ball. There was this woman, she bent over at one of the tables and her dress ripped down the side, the whole thing split open her Spanx on display for everyone to see. The funniest thing," Sadie says loud enough for everyone to hear, and the table erupts in small snickers.

Flames erupt in my chest, and all I want is for them to burn me alive so I'm reduced to nothing but a pile of ashes. Sadie wasn't even there for that, I didn't even know her then. I left getting a dress to the last minute and ended up wearing something from the back of my closet that fit five diets ago. It was risky to start with but there was no other choice. One wrong move and the threads finally gave out. I was mortified and left while holding my dress against my body to keep it up.

I remember Hallie laughing at me from her table.

"Oh my god," Sadie feigned surprise. "Wait a minute, wasn't that you Harper?"

My throat begins to burn in an instant.

This only solidifies that my sister feels nothing and maybe even hates me, despite not actually knowing anything about me.

Across from me both women wear matching smug faces as I wait for the ground to open up and swallow me. I didn't want to be here for a reason. I don't come back here because despite the blood we share, these people are not my family. I don't have a family, all I have is myself.

A heavy hand comes down on my thigh, causing me to jump. My head snaps to Nolan, and with the smallest movement possible, I shake my head and push his hand off.

"What's wrong, Harper, can't take a joke," Hallie mocks before faking a pout.

This is where a braver version of myself would stand up and tell her no, she just wasn't funny. The bolder version of me would get up and leave this house and never look back. But those versions of me don't exist yet, they're still trapped somewhere under all the optimism that lives inside of me, hoping for the day these people open their eyes and realize they aren't supposed to treat others this way.

"I'm sorry, I seem to have missed the joke," Nolan answers for me, practically stealing the words from my mouth. "All I heard was a snide story that's not funny."

Nolan's hand is back on me, gripping my thigh, the fabric of my skirt bunching in his hand while he challenges Sadie. Internal whiplash is taking over as I look from the devil twins across from me trying to force me out of this house and the man next to me lighting my skin on fire with a single touch.

With a flip, Sadie turns the mean girl persona off and turns on, what I think she thinks is a seductress, and points it toward Nolan. "Oh, we're just playing," she croons, and even throws in a wink for good measure.

I might vomit if I have to stay here any longer.

"Yeah, it's just a game, Harper knows she's not like us, it's fine," says Hallie

"Not like who?" Nolan pushes back clearly, not grasping onto what she's implying. What she always loves to remind me. That I don't belong.

"No, I'm sorry, you are going to have to spell it out for me because there's no way you're saying what I think you're saying, out loud and in front of people, to your sister."

"Nolan, please stop," I whisper.

When this man who I only have a sexual relationship with, who's shown me more kindness in sixty seconds than my family has shown me all year, looks at me again, I want to tell him it's no use, that she's always been like this. But I can't get the words out.

The room is dead silent, all eyes on the four of us.

Sadie looks to Hallie for help, clearly no plan for what to say next if someone were to speak up. Hallie answers for her. "I just mean, look around, and you tell me what's different about Harper."

I'm done waiting for the hole to swallow me up. My chair topples over from how fast I push back from the table. "Excuse me," I rush to say, avoiding all eyes that are glued to me as I make my exit. I race toward the front door, yanking my purse off the coat rack and barreling out into the cold night air, gasping for my next breath.

My hands press against my car door, dropping my head between my arms waiting for the shaking to stop. I don't even hear Nolan come up behind me only moments later.

"Hey, so that was in-fucking-sane," Nolan's voice comes from behind me.

Quickly, I brush the stray tears from my cheeks. "That was a normal Monday for them," I answer with a watery voice.

He looks confused and I'm sure it's because this beautiful, rich, successful man has never had someone look at him and think he's somehow less than a person all because of his size. Nolan's the type of large women fawn over and men spend hours in the gym trying to achieve.

"There's a reason I don't come to dinners, a reason why I don't get invited in the first place." My words are harsher than they needed to be. "My family has always made it clear that I am different from them, my sister is just much less subtle about it, and Sadie, I don't even know where the fuck she came from or why she's friends with Hallie, but it doesn't surprise me that she feels the same way."

"I don't get it," he says softly, moving softly toward me but something inside of me snaps.

"And you never will because you look like that," I say, waving my free hand down his body. "You look like a Greek statue sprung to life in a museum and walked out. For God's sake, they call you Eros at Midnights, so you tell me, what could you possibly know about having everyone in your life look down on you because the number on a scale is higher for me than them?" By the end of the sentence, I'm yelling, and I'm not sure who I'm pissed off at more.

My parents, for setting the standard that I can be treated differently, or my siblings, for blindly following in their footsteps.

Maybe even Sadie, who seems to have walked into my life with the sole purpose of reminding me that no one sees me. That I will never have men look at me the way they gawk at her.

Maybe I'm even mad at Nolan, although I have no right to be. Sure, he stood up to Sadie and Hallie, and I didn't expect him to announce to the table that we're sleeping together, but something about the whole interaction felt off. He could touch me below the table but not in front of them. He can stand up for me, not because he thinks I'm beautiful, but because what they were saying was nasty. He can do all of that and then come after me only to say he didn't get it.

Somewhere along the way, I forgot we were nothing to each other. Nothing but a ticking countdown. There was nothing more between us. I wasn't his girlfriend, I wasn't even his friend. I was some girl he picked up at a sex club, who he likes to fuck in private and ignore in public.

"I get that I'm nothing to you outside the bedroom," I say, "but you just sat there while they berated me. How do you think that makes me feel?" I question him, not really wanting to know the answer because if he says what I think he will, then everything between us will end.

He looks as if I struck him across the face, the way his head rears back and his eyes dance with a painful look. "Harper, I..."

That's all he said. Anything that might have followed died in the wind between us.

In my heart, I knew we were always going to reach a point where one of us got our fill of the other and I'll be damned if I'm going to be the one on the chopping block first.

This was never going to last—even if for a moment I thought we had something bigger than all the lessons, there was no way anything between us could ever work. The deal we struck was reaching its time limit and maybe it would be best if I ran down the clock until we slowly drift apart and back to what we were before the lessons, before the connection and the desire that burns between us.

"I'll see you at work."

I'm turning away from him and in my car within seconds and my heart aches that he did nothing to try and stop me.

CHAPTER SIXTEEN

FEBRUARY 10

You can only float in the clouds for so long before falling through the mist and plummeting to the ground. I wanted to believe Nolan and I could be more, it felt like we were on our way to being bigger than those stupid lessons. But the part that cuts the deepest is I'm not even surprised.

And if falling through the mist of clouds wasn't enough, I was heading straight into a world on fire.

"What do you mean?" My voice pierces through the receiver and the longer the silence draws on, the further down I spiral.

The woman lets out a heavy breath. "I'm sorry, Ms. Hawthorne, but your assistant called three days ago and canceled the band."

"That's impossible. I don't even have an assistant. I'm in charge of the event, and I never called in. Why would I even do that?"

Air crackles over the line. "I don't know, Ma'am."

"It's in four days, what am I supposed to do?" Tears blur my vision. I have to tilt my head back with the phone against my ear to keep them from spilling over.

It's one thing after another, and I'm on the verge of snapping. The rentals being double booked was an easy enough fix but losing the band right before the event is impossible to fix.

Am I cursed? Is that what's happening? Someone, somewhere decided I've been having too much fun losing myself in Nolan and decided I now must be punished for it.

"Okay, okay." There's nothing really left for me to say and hang up the phone.

I hang up the phone and my head drops with a loud thud onto my desk. Never mind the pain when my world is imploding. There's absolutely no coming back from this, not even a miracle can save me from the disaster that's going to be The Cupid's Ball. If the table runners were missing, most people wouldn't even know. But no band, that was something everyone will notice and talk about until my mistake is this towns' biggest celebrity.

This is what a downhill spiral must feel like, but when will the bottom appear? Between last night and being told the band was canceled, I honestly don't know which hurts worse.

I wanted to believe Nolan and I were creating something deeper, something organic that might last beyond whatever expiration date was on our arrangement but now it's evident we're just too different to work. No matter how much you shake it, oil and water separate in the end.

My creaking office door catches my attention but I don't even bother lifting my head. My world is ending and I'm fine wallowing in my melodramatics for now.

"Sleeping on the job is a bit tacky, don't you think?"

I don't have to open my eyes to know my sister is standing in my office. But why on Earth is she here? Our father's been mayor for the last twenty years and I don't think she's ever willingly set foot in City Hall.

Reluctantly, I peel my cheek off the wooden desk. "What are you doing here, Hallie?" Locking eyes with a woman who, despite our differences, looks almost the same as me. It's a bit eerie, knowing she hates all that I am.

"Came to see Sadie."

"And since when do you know Sadie anyway?"

She rolls her eyes. "Years, how do you think she got the job? Daddy said Nolan needed a new secretary and who better than Sadie?"

That actually makes me laugh. "Literally anyone would be better than Sadie," I mutter under my breath.

Hallie hovers in the doorway.

"Well she doesn't work in here so feel free to go find her."

"You and Nolan seem to be close?" She takes a step further into the room.

"He's my boss." I'm not sure if she can sense the tremor in my voice but if Hallie's here and questioning me about Nolan, it's not good. My stomach twists at the thought.

"Pretty nice of your *boss* to come to your defense last night. Even left the table to go check on you."

"Where are you going with this?"

Another step toward me and a sinister smile graces her face and her eyes go dead. "Whatever's going on between you two, end it."

The twister in my stomach takes off cause how the fuck does she know. "I'm not sure what you're talking about."

"Oh, please, Nolan couldn't take his eyes off of you all night and then after that little display of chivalry, it was easy to put together. Tell me, does Daddy know you're sleeping with his best friend?"

"Thats nobody's business."

"It's my business," she snaps.

I rise from my desk, shaking fingers pressing into the desk. "Why? What's it to you, Hallie?"

I expect her to give me some shallow reason about why I should call it off. Something about Sadie being a better match. Instead, her face slowly hardens. "Leave Nolan alone."

"Or what, Hallie?" I throw my arms up. "What will you do? Ruin my life? Newsflash, you've been doing that since we were kids, three decades of being tortured or ignored by you, so why would this be any different?"

"Oh, please, Harper, you're so quick to act the victim. Grow up."

"Are you kidding me?" My feet move on their own, walking around my desk and to Hallie until our shoes are practically touching.

My whole life I've been waiting for my tipping point. The point in my life where I finally grew a backbone and stood up for myself, although I'm surprised the motivator is being told to stay away from Nolan. A lifetime of being told I'm not good enough should have toppled me into a well I can't climb out of, but it didn't, it merely sent me running from everything in Cupid, my family included.

And then I found Nolan—the one person who sees me the way I see myself. A capable woman. A woman worth a life full of love, passion, and fun. If they think they're going to take him away from me, they're wrong.

"You know what, Hallie? I feel sorry for you. You've lived your life under the heavy thumb of our parents and this town and lost your brain in the process. You can't even think for yourself and it's pathetic."

Hallie simply scoffs, but there's a shift in her eyes telling me I was approaching a sore spot.

"I'm sorry that you feel the need to come here and do our father's dirty work for whatever he's got planned, but you don't know me, and you don't know Nolan, so I'm going to say this once, and then I hope I never talk to you again. I am fucking Nolan, I don't care who knows and I sure as hell am not going to stay away from him."

"You may not care who knows, but I'm sure Nolan does. Why else wouldn't he tell Dad about you two last night after you left?"

"Get the fuck out of my office."

A slow smile unfurls across her face and a sickening feeling crawls up my throat. "That's all I needed to know."

Was this what she wanted all along? For me to confirm out loud that Nolan and I are involved? I don't move, I won't give anything away but I want to double over and empty my stomach on the floor the longer she looks at me. And the feeling only worsens when Nolan appears behind her in the doorway.

"Harper?" he questions, eyes spinning from me to Hallie. He moves around her and into my office. "Everything okay?"

The room empties, the atmosphere gone, sucking us into a vacuum of tension. Hallie answers for us, turning her persona of the perfect Cupid Sweetheart back on. "Of course, I just stopped by to see my little sister before going to lunch with Sadie."

Even Nolan can taste the lie. "Uh-huh," he hums, stepping closer to me.

Hallie zones in on the minuscule movement, the prize she was waiting for. "Well I better get going, and Harper, don't forget that Dad always gets what he wants. Whether we like it or not." She turns, dark hair whipping around with her body and her heels click against the hard floor as she disappears.

"What does that mean?" Nolan's voice breaks through my reeling mind.

She's right though. There's never been a time where my father didn't get his way, it's how he's remained Mayor of Cupid for so long. He's not above blackmail or intimidation to pave his path. If my father needs Nolan, it's because of one thing, the only thing he has that my father doesn't—money. I just don't know where Sadie fits into the equation.

"Baby?" Quiet concern coats Nolan's words.

I snap back and step away as his hand ghosts along my back.

"Don't." My head's reeling. "Nolan, I can't, I—"

He tilts his head to the side, confused as a puppy who doesn't understand why you leave every day, and I can see the moment my words slice through his normal suit of stoic armor. Cracks form along the outline, his eyes bore into me and in my hands I hold all this power over a powerful man. I don't want to hurt him, but I can't think when he's in front of me.

"Nolan, I can't do this right now. I need some space."

Watching him crumble as the words hit him is not something I can handle. But what's worse is how fast he picks up his pieces.

He nods somberly, "I understand."

Nolan turns and follows Hallie's steps from moments before.

So this is what crashing into a burning world feels like.

CHAPTER SEVENTEEN

Nolan

FEBRUARY 12

I'M STANDING IN FRONT of Harper's apartment door without a plan. Not even an inkling of what I want to say to her but I was pulled here by some unknown feeling that wants me to spill my guts to her. She's been a ghost the past two days. Barely answering my texts, doing whatever she can to not be in the same room as me at work, and it's slowly killing me.

I'm consumed by Harper and I don't want to stop. It's more than sex, it's more than any physical pleasure she pulls from my body. It's bigger than our dynamic, and deeper than anything I thought I could find or deserve.

In my fifty-two years on this earth, I've spent most of them alone. Filling my time with work, a few friends and more passing flings than I can even recall and all of it was fine. I was fine. I built a life I was comfortable dying in while the world moved around me, and the idea of love never crossed my mind.

Until Harper. And now she's the only thing occupying my mind.

Muffled footsteps come from inside once I finally draw the courage to knock. When the door swings open, I don't quite know what I'm looking at. Most of my time with her is spent at work, when she's styled in a way that meets all the business standards and yet still hangs onto her whimsical aura. Her hair is usually in soft curls or tied nicely at the nape of her neck. She wears such little make up, I would never think to be shocked to see her without it.

But I am.

Because she's not just dressed down for a night at home, her entire appearance looks like she's straddling the edge of frazzled and a full on breakdown.

I can't even get a breath out before she bursts into tears and buries her head in her hands. Without an invitation, I rush through the door, scooping her in my arms and kick the door shut.

"Baby, what happened?" I asked, ready to avenge her, like a knight with a sword at the helm, for whatever or whoever did her wrong. Her only answer is a choking sob against my chest.

With a slight bend, I scoop her up, cradling her against my chest and look for the couch. I've never been here before but Harper seems to live like any other average twenty-five year old.

Falling carefully into the couch, I grip Harper tighter as to not let her slip off my lap. It takes a couple adjustments but soon enough she's cradled in my arm, face still buried into the front of my shirt, soft cries still coming. And I feel utterly helpless.

I don't know what to do. I don't even know where to start. There's never been a time I've felt the need to fix all the wrongs in the world for one single person, and I'm afraid if I prod her with questions, it will only make it worse.

So I don't say a word. My arms grip her tight to my body as I press my check against the silky strands of the hair piled on top of her head.

And I wait.

It's amazing the things you can learn about someone from just their home. If I walked into five homes blindly, I would still guess this one would belong to Harper. Warmth oozes from every corner, seeping into your skin the longer you stay. Art decorates every wall, prints and canvases, some that look as if she drew them herself, making it seem as if we've landed into a museum and not a living room.

It's all her, every inch.

Minutes tick by and with each one that passes, her breathing evens out, and she melts deeper into my arms. It's a feeling unlike anything I've ever encountered and all at once, it's like a missing piece of me quietly slides into place.

I love her.

I love her, and I want this. This moment where I'm her comfort, every day. Every day for the rest of my days.

Harper stirs. Her face is still pressing into my chest when I look down at her. "Do you want to talk about it?" I ask. Her next breath is heavy, warming where her lips are pressed against me and a weak answer is muffled by my shirt

"No."

I brush a few fallen tendrils of hair back so I can see her. One eye peels open and looks up.

"It can't be that bad."

"I've ruined everything."

"Everyone makes mistakes but I doubt you ruined anything."

Harper sits up in my lap. "What do you know about making mistakes? You're perfect." Her face screws into a glare when I laugh. I lean forward and place a kiss against her cheek, and then the other until her face softens.

"I wish that was the truth, Sweet Girl, but I am the furthest thing from perfect."

She huffs out in disbelief, rolling her eyes as she does. "I called the manager of the band I scheduled months ago to confirm they had everything for Saturday and they told me, my assistant called and canceled them a few days ago."

"What?"

She expels a large breath. "I don't know how it happened, or why, but I didn't call to cancel and there was nothing I could do to get back on their books. It's like someone is sabotaging me." Anxiety pushes her voice up an octave as she talks. "I don't know what to do. I've ruined the ball, which helps so many departments which I've now also ruined. Maybe you're not perfect but I doubt you've ever nearly taken down a town with your job."

"Have I told you why I'm here, in Cupid?"

A few of the coiled tendrils framing her face shake with her head. The story isn't even shocking, but it sits in my chest and I've been walking around with this shameful medal since I got here. My fingers slip up and down her leggings, a soothing pattern that was initially for her but now it's the only thing tethering me to this moment.

Harper is the least selfish person I've met, I doubt that once she finds out, she'll leap from my lap and cast me from her house, but I hook my hands around her hips as if that will keep her here anyway.

"I've belonged to Midnights since it began, before it even began. I gave Maxine the start-up funds to open the place," I begin, brushing my thumb along the sliver of skin showing between her bottoms and the small tank top.

"You know Maxine?"

There's an unmistakable infliction in her voice. "Not like that. Maxine and I are friends, and only friends. We met in business school. She came from a family where she had to work nights and weekends, with no days off to even afford school, and I obviously had money to spare. I don't remember how we found out each of us preferred a certain *type* in the bedroom but as a gift for her one of her birthdays and for myself I gave her the funds to start Midnights."

"And you two have never been together?"

I laugh at the skeptical glimmer rolling through her eyes like a slow fog as she leans back, glowering in my direction. Maxine is beautiful so I don't fault her for asking, but even if Harper doesn't see it, I belong to her and only her. "Never, we're friends only. Besides, Maxine is a lot like me in the bedroom, and that can be challenging to say the least."

"What does Midnights have to do with your job?"

"Exactly what I asked my father when he found out that not only am I a silent partner for a sex club, but that I also frequent said sex club." She shifts on my lap and while I want to push into her flesh and keep her, I'd never force her to stay. "My father didn't like that the board edged him out as CEO when he turned seventy and then appointed me. He told me that if I stepped down quietly, he wouldn't leak to whatever press outlet would listen, how I'm a sexual deviant who likes to prey on helpless women in order to control them."

A soft gasp falls from her mouth and her warm, earthy eyes widen. An outpouring of relief runs through me. As if someone was finally seeing it from my point of view. "He did not," she whispers.

"Unfortunately, he did. My first thought was to call his bluff but something like that could not only ruin everything I've built for myself, but it could ruin the company, and worse it could destroy everything Maxine worked for. If it was just me, then I probably would have told him to shove it and deal with the consequences but I couldn't let my proclivities bring down the people around me."

"He had no right. What you do in the bedroom is nobody's business but yours and whoever willingly consents to being with you. Just because you like things a particular way, doesn't make you a bad person."

"Doesn't it, though?"

Her head tilts to the side, eyes pinging around my face with a softness I've grown to crave. "I don't understand," she says, and I wish I never opened my mouth at all, because what if this is where I lose her?

"But what if he's right?" I approach the question as I would a wounded jungle cat, ready for the answer to destroy me.

"I'm not helpless, Nolan." Her voice immediately defensive.

"I know."

"And you don't control me."

"I know."

" I can say no or stop or leave at any time."

"Of course you can. I don't want to control you, I never wanted that."

"So fuck him." She's smug when she says it.

My head rears back as the words burst through her perfect lips. I'm not sure I've ever heard Harper curse. The vulgar sound is harsh coming from her but pulls a laugh deep from my chest.

"I'm serious. What we have or are doing is no one's business and even if it was, it's not wrong, so fuck him for thinking he can try and out you to get what he wants."

"Are you sure you're real?" I muse out loud as I press forward and capture her lips with mine. It's a tender action, millions of miles away from our usual embraces but feels intricately right.

A heavy sigh crawls up her throat at the first touch, and I swallow it down, hungry for anything she gives me. Because she's right. Fuck him. Harper was never someone to control, or someone I tricked into my bed. I presented an option, she said yes, and it immediately became a privilege to be with her.

But I want more. So much more. I yearn for her obedience, but I need *her* more.

My arms circle around her waist, and one hand snakes up her spine and into her hair as I deepen the kiss. Exploring with my tongue as her jaw drops open with a heavy pant, allowing me to slip through. It's the kind of sound a man can get drunk on, one simple noise and my head is the clouds.

"I want you," she says on an exhale, breath dripping with sweet desperation. She could ask for anything, and I know I could never deny her.

"You have me, Harper," I confess, not even scared, that for once, I've told the truth. I don't care about what the fallout may be from my words, if she'll have me, I'll spend the rest of my life devoted to her.

Her hips roll, the friction is almost unbearable. Unbridled heat radiates from between her thighs, drowning me in warmth I want to wrap myself in. She does it again and a slight whine fills her chest that my cock responds to, hardening to a painful threshold in my slacks.

"You like that, Sweet Girl?"

Her head lolls in a slow nod as she continues to rock back and forth.

"Use me, Harper," my words strain, already on an edge. "Rub your needy cunt on me, make a mess of me."

She rocks back and forth, the thin fabric growing wetter with every slow passing. "What's the lesson for tonight?"

She mumbles against my lip, sliding her arms around my neck, pulling me closer.

"No lesson, just you and me, baby."

She pulls back, searching my face. There's a million things I can say to her right now but that's not what she needs.

Without a word, she moves like water, pliable and willing as I guide one of her legs over my thigh. It's not enough, not nearly enough for what I want to give her.

"Are you particularly attached to these?" My voice rattles with want as I skim my fingertips along the waistband of her leggings.

I love that she answers without pause. "No, Sir."

Thin fabric rips like tissue paper, exposing her to me. Harper sucks in a sharp breath. Under her leggings, she's completely bare. Bare, glistening, and perfect. I guide her down onto my thigh, until she's enveloping me in a heat I'll gladly die in.

"Take what you need, baby."

Harper's hands press against my shoulders, fingers intertwining with the fabric, and slowly tilts her hips, dragging her center along my thigh.

Shudders rattle our chests simultaneously. My head falls back to the couch as hers dips forward to press against my chest. "Do it again," I strain to say, barely hanging on by a thread.

She pulls back and rocks forward again. "Yes, Sir," she breathes and I feel the smile playing on her lips.

I've died and gone to heaven. If there was anything past heaven, I would have transcended there as well. Harper is relentless, picking up speed, slowing down and rolling her hips into me with abandon. Without shame. She takes what she wants, rubbing her slick, wet cunt against my leg, whimpering for more with each stroke.

"That's my girl."

With her head thrown back, each labored breath has her breasts straining to stay contained in the tight, thin strapped shirt she has on. "Am I? Am I your girl, Sir?"

My fingers thread into the hair along her neck as I crash my mouth into hers. Desperate to show her exactly how much she is mine and how much I am hers. Harper's lips meet mine with as much fervor as I was pouring into her. Her mouth is as sweet and soft as cotton candy as I run my tongue along her bottom lip, nipping at the reddened flesh.

"You must think I'm terrible." I pant as she grinds harder and faster. "For not telling you every second, of every fucking day, that you're mine." I'm unable to stop myself from meeting each rock of her hips.

My cock weeps in my pants, a ludicrous amount of pre-cum coating the inside of my boxers and my own climax barreling to the surface. I haven't came in my pants since I was a pre-teen but I'll quickly have to adjust that streak, because with Harper using me to chase her orgasm, I'm minutes away from spilling all over myself.

She whines as I bury my face in her chest, pawing at her top until tits are free and hanging heavy with need. "So fucking perfect." My tongue darts out, licking a stripe across her right breast, pulling back only long enough to say, "So fucking mine." Harper cries out my name and a slough of profanities follow when my lips latch onto her hardened nipple and she arches into me. "And I'll tell you every day."

Her hips grind down harder, fingers dig into my shoulder as she tips over the edge. My dick pulses, and I lose my battle with trying not to finish as my climax washes over me, heavier than a tsunami wave.

We stay locked in a tight embrace as we float back down from the clouds, as she toys with the hair on the back of my neck, her head resting on my shoulder.

I'm not sure she even realizes it as she drifts off but her last words, as faint as they are, are clear. "I'm yours, Nolan."

CHAPTER EIGHTEEN

FEBRUARY 13

IN NO WORLD WOULD Harper cancel the band before the ball and it wasn't hard to figure out who was behind it. That particular problem would be handled later because I have one day to pull a miracle out of my ass.

Harper fell asleep curled into my side as I lay awake trying to figure out how to help.

The only issue is I don't know a damn thing about hiring a band. But what I do have is an almost limitless amount of money to make things happen, and for Harper I was going to make sure tomorrow went on as planned. And I have Maxine. With those two things at my disposal, there's not much I can't accomplish.

I could have just called her but this might be something I need to beg for and it would be better to do in person. Not that Maxine will withhold any help from me, but I haven't seen or talked to her since I chased after Harper running out of Midnights.

During the day Midnights is simply a building in an industrial park. Few vendors come in and out every day; cleaners, beverage sellers who stock the bar, and a laundry service. Maxine even has a contract with a local upscale sex store that stops by once a month to make sure all the toys are still in working shape and the Shibari ropes aren't fraying. Maxine has a contact for everything.

I punch the code into the door since the bodyguard doesn't start until the sun sets, and head straight to Maxine's office.

The door's slightly a jar, I knock once before pushing into her office. Maxine's head snaps up, surprise flashes in her eye first at the sudden intrusion she wasn't expecting before she splits into a smile. "Nolan, what are you doing here?"

"Hey, Max." I drop into one of the chairs in front of her.

She stops whatever she was doing on her computer and gives me her full attention. There's a million reasons to like Maxine, but my favorite attribute has to be that she will always give you her full attention. Doesn't matter if you show up unannounced, or if she was in the middle of a conference call, if you call in need, Maxine is always there. "Uh oh, what's wrong?" There's also never any use in lying to her because she always knows when something's wrong.

Suddenly the band is the last thing on my mind. "Did you invite Harper to Midnights for me?"

She laughs affectionately. "The world does not revolve around you, Nolan, despite what you were taught growing up."

"I'm serious, Maxine."

"And so am I. I knew who Harper was. You moved to Cupid and then all the sudden every other sentence was about her. 'Dan's daughter Harper works for me', 'I wish everyone worked as hard as Harper', 'Harper mentioned a gallery here in the city, we should check it out', I don't even think you realized how much you talked about her."

Flames in my chest lick up my neck. I pull on my collar trying to get any type of breeze to cool this embarrassment down. Because she's right, I didn't know I talked about her at all.

"Harper applied for the open house night all on her own, I only knew because I went through every application. Then you found her before I could introduce you two. You're trying to give me too much credit and normally I would bask in the glory but I did nothing, you two were simply—" she shrugs a single shoulder, "kismet."

"Kismet?"

Now I know she's fucking with me. How can Harper and I be destined to be together? Doesn't make much sense since we've known each other for...well I don't even really like to think about it because technically, I've known her since she was born.

I slump into the chair a bit further. "I don't think that's the best word to describe what we are."

"Then what would you call it?"

"I don't—" I shift around in the chair a bit. "What if—"

There's a thousand thoughts swirling in my head, and I know I can spill them all to Maxine without judgment but I still can't get them to come out. If they come out that might make them real and I prefer to keep my insecurities to myself.

"Spit it out." Maxine's tone is a touch bored.

"I can't give her what she deserves." I shout a bit louder than I need to

A burst of air blows past Maxine lips, her dark eyes rolling at my outburst. "That's absurd, you are Nolan Archer, there is nothing you can't give her. Nice try."

"I can't give her time, and it wouldn't be fair to her." Her head tilts to the side and clearly I'm going to have to spell this out for her. "I am twenty-two years older than her."

I can't bring myself to look at her, and I almost missed her near silent 'oh'. Instead, I stare at the picture of Eros on her wall. I gave it to her as a gift for opening Midnights as a joke. So she could always think of me, since she was the one to give me the name Eros. But Maxine liked it so much she kept it and hung it in her office.

"Have you asked Harper what she wants?" When I don't answer, she continues on. "Of course not, because that would be too easy. Nolan, you are the best person I know, and for years I've watched you self sabotage every relationship you've dipped your toes into for reasons I'll never fully comprehend. You deserve good things and Harper is a good thing."

"And what happens in ten years when I'm an AARP member, retired and waiting on Medicare to pay for my medical treatment? In twenty years, when it's harder for me to walk around and need a hip replacement and she's forced to take care of me while she is still young and in her prime?"

"First of all, you're never going to be an AARP member or use Medicare, you're literally a millionaire, why would you need it?" she says while grinning at me but when I don't join in on her humor, her face switches. "I've never seen you like this over a woman, or anyone. You must really like her."

She's a hard person to surprise but Maxine's eyes double in size as my next words kind of tumble out. "I love her, and I feel like if I tell her, I'm saddling her with a life that will only bring her down."

Her recovery is quick. "You're an idiot. Stop making decisions for your future and talk to Harper, see what she says because I can guarantee none of that will matter to her, because *you* matter to her."

"I hate when you are right."

"I know." Her face, smug. "Is this really what you came all the way out here for? To spill the inner workings of your heart to me?"

Right, the band.

"No, actually, I need a band." She immediately reaches for her phone, and I thank whatever God will listen, because I must have done something good in my life to have a friend like Maxine. "I can pay whatever but I have no clue where to start looking."

"Keep your wallet in your pants," she says without looking up, thumbs flying over her phone. "I have a cousin in Cornelia whose son is in a band."

"Are they good?"

She shrugs. "Define good?"

"Maxine, I need the band to at least be decent."

"Calm down, they can play. I'll just tell them to stick to covers, their original stuff isn't quite what you're looking for probably."

"Thanks, Max, you're the best."

"I know."

Could the band suck? Maybe. Probably most definitely, but what other options do I have? At least I can give Harper this. It may not be much, and it may not mean anything to her but I couldn't sit back and do nothing. I would move mountains for Harper, rope the heavens and lay them at her feet. And if she lets me, I will willingly take whatever amount of time she'll give me and live my life for her.

CHAPTER NINETEEN

FEBRUARY 14

Skipping town was the first thought on my mind. There's a bag packed, waiting on my bed and everything. I don't know where I'll go, there's not a single corner of this state where my father won't be able to find me. And when he shows up, realizes there's no band and that it's just me in a corner with a playlist for tonight's ball—well, I don't really want to think about it. Because while my father may not like to acknowledge me, this is one fuck up I'm sure he'll make a scene about.

I reached out to every event planner in Northern California for resources. I combed through social media, looking for anything remotely resembling a band for tonight, and came up empty. Not even a Tesla cover band was available. I was ready to swallow my pride and beg Nolan to pay some exorbitant fee for a last minute DJ but there was no point because *no one* was available.

It's like the universe was toying with me. How many parties and events could there possibly be tonight that everyone is booked? At least if my father murders me, it will be in a lavish event space and I'll look phenomenal.

For a moment while getting ready, I contemplated not even putting on the dress Nolan bought. As if denying myself the simple pleasure of wearing it makes up for my colossal screw up. There were a few drab looking black dresses hanging in the back of my closet I could have worn instead, but for some reason my heart ached while looking at the deep red gown laid out on my bed. In the end, the organ in my chest won.

Of course it fits like a glove. Of course after slipping into my heels and lining my lips with a matching shade of red,

I looked at myself and felt beautiful. And of course Nolan was the first person I thought of once I was ready.

And I hated how much I wanted to show him. Because soon Nolan will walk through the ballroom doors, along with half the town, and we won't be anything to each other. Despite anything we might have said the other night. Meaningless words whispered in a moment that faded away with the stars. A fluke in time because when I woke in the morning, he was gone.

I'm wallowing in my own self pity, walking around the table, adjusting silverware that was already straight, when a voice comes from behind me.

"Excuse me, Ma'am, do you know where we're supposed to set up?"

Guests aren't meant to show up for another thirty minutes and as far as I know, all the vendors are accounted for. Cupid is so small that I genuinely know what everyone looks like and even if I didn't, the man standing before me is someone I would remember. With his ice blonde hair tousled with lazy precision and haunting blue eyes. This sudden stranger appears to have walked off a runway, straight into this ballroom and I can't for the life of me figure out why.

"I'm sorry, but we're not expecting any more vendors. What are you here for?"

The mystery man twists to the side, looking around the room as if it's obvious why he's here. Only then do I register the guitar strapped to his back. He looks back to me, apprehension splashed across his face. "I'm Ryker, my band just needs to know where to set up."

Thank Cupid, it's a Valentine's Day miracle.

My brain rattles as I sputter and shake my head looking for something to say. "I don't know—I—how—"

"We just need to know where to set up, Ma'am."

Three more men walk into the room, all with instruments strapped to them or equipment being rolled on a cart. I have no idea where they came from but I'm not stupid enough to turn them away. I gesture toward the stage, and in record time they're set up, and different chords are ringing throughout the room as they run a sound check.

Even though I'm smiling ear to ear so hard my cheeks hurt, I feel as if I might actually cry.

"Have I told you how much I love your smile," a familiar timbre says from behind me. My body flushes, his presence pulling a reaction from me before I can even turn to look at him. When I swirl around, the satin train of my dress spinning out with me, I'm almost knocked off my heels at the sight of him.

Nolan's suit is darker than a velvety midnight sky, his piercing blue eyes the only color on him. Tiny crinkles deepen around his eyes as his lips unfurl in a slow smile as he drags his gaze down my body. "You look beautiful, Harper."

Before I can answer, another voice cuts through. "Hey, Nolan, right?" Ryker calls out as he jumps off the stage and struts over to us. Nolan pulls me back and tucks me into his side, resting a heavy hand on my hip. A small move with an inescapable message; I'm his.

The two men shake hands and I'm left a bit bewildered.

"Thank you so much for giving us a chance, we really appreciate it."

"No problem, Maxine said you're good and that's all we needed to know. This is Harper, she's the Director of Recreations in Cupid and put on this whole event." Ryker quickly shakes my hand and I barely get out a 'thank you' before he's heading back to the stage to finish setting up.

I turn to Nolan. "How—"

"There's yet to be a problem Maxine can't solve. I drove out to see her yesterday and begged for help."

"But why?"

His next statement came quickly but not a word was rushed. It was a steady proclamation, the kind that sticks with you years down the road. The moment you know changes everything. "There's nothing I wouldn't do for you, Harper."

Reality slips away at his words.

My entire life, I've weaved in and out of people's lives, stealing glimpses of what it's like to be wanted and keeping them for myself. Tucking little pieces of what it's like to have somebody into my back pocket because I never knew when it would be my turn. I've spent so long trying to do everything myself with no one to lean on and here he was, helping me when I didn't even ask. Offering me the soft landing I've been dreaming of.

A lifetime spent wondering why no one was on my side, and with his one simple statement, Nolan unties all of my self doubt, letting it fall from my shoulders like a discarded cloak.

One sentence from him and I want to spill my heart's secrets and bargain with the devil to let me keep him.

"I don't know what to say," I say, my voice, breathless. Behind me a faint chatter grows louder as guests start to wander in. The lights dim, signaling the night is about to begin but all I want is more time in this small snow globe of a moment.

"Harper, I—"

"Nolan." My father's voice booms across the ballroom and the moment slips away.

Before Nolan turns to him, his fingertips sweep down my forearm. "I should go. "

I nod, and then he's gone.

My feet ache, my cheeks burn from smiling, and my heart is so full I can barely stand it. Every minute that's passed since Nolan walked away has been flawless. Each person I've talked raved; about the decor, the band, and of course the amount of money we've raised for the town.

The band, who I now know is called Gravestone Odyssey, is incredible. From what I've picked up they're a rock back from a few towns over, who normally perform their own songs that have a lot more screaming in them. Which I'm sure is great, but I'm thankful they've stuck to covers for the night.

Nolan has been elusive; I've caught glimpses of him throughout the night and each time I do, his eyes are already on me. I'm dying to know what he was going to say before my father arrived. I'm trailing along the border of the dance floor when the music switches and a softer melody streams out of the speakers.

I'm watching all the couples slow down, women draping their arms around necks and men slipping arms around waists when suddenly a hand slips into mine and I'm being pulled out onto the floor.

My gasp lets out into a soft breath when I register Nolan's hand in mine. "What are we doing, Nolan?" I lean in to whisper, letting my hand fall from his grasp. Or at least I tried to.

He holds me tighter. The room spins as I'm twirled around and brought closer into his chest. "Dancing," he answers.

My eyes dart around but no one seems to notice or care. "But, people will see."

"That's never been an issue for me." His voice is tender and the words are more genuine than I've ever heard.

Relaxing into his arms is a move that requires no thought, a muscle movement developed over only two weeks. A movement heavy with realization of finding a safe place to fall and all the regret of knowing I won't have it for long. But I think I'm okay with it, because this is what I wanted out of this whole glorious mess; to feel wanted.

With the warmth of Nolan's hands sinking through the fabric of my dress and his cheek pressing gently against the top of my head I have everything I could possibly want.

The lead singer croons the words of a Cigarettes After Sex song in turn with hollow snare drum taps and deep reverberating bass guitar. I'm lulled into a hazy state I never want to come out of. "This is nice." My voice, as dreamy as my thoughts.

Nolan's chest expands under my face as I press further into him. "I could stay here forever, Sweet Girl." His lips press against my hair as he murmurs the words but there's no mistaking what he said.

When his throat bobs with a thick swallow, and his body stills under my touch, I zip up my feelings that were oozing out moments ago. This is not the stature of a man who is about to give me good news. Despite his sentiment.

"Harper, I'm twenty two years older than you," he says as if it's a way to explain away what's about to happen.

I breathe out. "I know."

"I'm your boss."

"I know." My heart turns to lead in my chest.

We stop dancing and he gazes down at me but there's no remorse in his eyes. "And I've been your dad's friend for years."

I can feel it, the last nail in the coffin, the one that was always coming but I was all too happy ignoring it. He's going to tell me we're through, that whatever arrangement we have is at its end and will let me down gently because he's kind and would never want to hurt me.

Bracing myself for the inevitable blow, I pull back from his chest but his hands grip me around the waist and keep me from moving.

Nolan's eyes search mine. Straining, pleading, yearning. A vast spectrum of emotions encapsulated in the prettiest glacier blue orbs.

"Everything is telling me it's not fair to want more with you, that you have your whole life in front of you and I would only become a burden." The distraught tone of his voice sinks into my skin, as if his head and heart are pulling him in different directions. "But I can't help it. I love you, Harper, and I want so much more than what we already have together."

Trembling starts in the tips of my fingers before working its way up arms under every inch of skin. It's like I've forgotten how to speak. His confession kickstarted a reboot of my mind and left me with a blank screen.

Nolan Archer loves me.

Me.

He loves *me*.

I run through the statement in my head in a million different variations because I can't believe it. My nervous system was ready for rejection, it shut itself down so the pain of being left would minimize whatever damage his words were going to cause because I was sure I loved him, and that would have wrecked me.

Couples twirl around us, casting conspiring glances as we interrupt the flow of the dance floor by remaining still.

The longer I take to answer, concern grows larger in his eyes but right as I open my mouth to tell him exactly how I feel, my parents spin by us.

My mother takes one look at my gown and downturns her thin pale pink painted lips. Her eyes narrow on my bust line, silently critiquing.

"Nolan, thanks for taking one for the team, but I'm sure Harper is needed somewhere and Sadie's been waiting all night for you to ask her to dance."

There's a shift in the air between us. Nolan stands a bit taller, rolling his shoulders back as his features morphed into a scowl.

"I'm right where I want to be."

My father's laugh is an exasperated bark. "Funny, I think she's sitting at the table." He then turns to me. "Harper, you can go."

As helpless as a feather caught in the wind, I follow his dismissal. My foot steps out to leave when fingers thread through mine with a tight grasp.

"Harper's also exactly where she needs to be."

I watch as my father's eyes slide from Nolan to me, and then to where our hands are still joined. "What is going on?" My father doesn't even try to keep the accusatory tone out of his voice. It's front and center, demanding access to information he has no business knowing.

A lie is slowly loading on the tip of my tongue but Nolan speaks first. "Harper and I have been seeing each other."

My mother gasps, in an honest to God, pearl clutching moment. I have to force my eyes shut or else they'll roll into the back of my head. As if the mere thought of us as a couple would cause her to faint.

"You and Harper?" Dad questions, slowly drawing his eyes from Nolan, to me, and then to where Nolan has his arm draped across my waist. "But she's so..."

I'm all too familiar with the feeling lighting up in my gut and anticipating the next words out of my father's mouth. Too big, too plain, too much and not enough all at the same time.

My spine turns to lead but Nolan only grips me tighter.

"Dan, we've been friends a long time." Nolan's words are quick to cut off whatever my father was about to say.

"Yeah, longer than she's been alive," he interjects.

"But I won't hear a word about Harper from you or your family ever again. Either in front of me or behind our backs." Nolan drop his hands from mine, taking a step toward my parents. My mother is forced to tilt her head back and places herself behind her husband like it will do any good. Nolan and my father are the same height but the slight fear in his eyes isn't hard to miss from where I am. "I know what you've been doing."

My father doesn't respond. He only stares, a slight tick in his jaw after a second.

People are still moving around us. No one stops to see what's happening but I can feel all their eyes on us. Nolan doesn't care, he continues on. "I know about Sadie and her father. I also know that Apollo Enterprises rejected your initial proposal to fund your little expansion project."

My father tenses, shoulders rolling back and opening his mouth like he might say something but Nolan presses forward. "All I want is what's best for Cupid. The expansion is a good thing."

"Whatever deal you made with Sadie has emboldened her to try and sabotage this whole event for God knows what reason, but it stops now. All of it."

"Sadie?" I question; a thousand thoughts rushing in.

Nolan looks toward me. More and more eyes are on us, stopping to watch what's unfolding on the dance floor, but he doesn't seem to care. His fingers brush across my cheek, tucking a rogue curl behind my ear before dancing down my neck. One small move and I almost forgot the sea of people around us.

"I did some digging last night. The order that was double booked with ours was for Apollo Enterprises, Sadie's father's company, but there's no party. I checked her office phone records, and the band's management company was on her call log."

An amused laugh escapes me. "Why am I not surprised?"

Nolan smiles, bending closer, his lips in each when my father clears his throat. Nolan follows through anyway, pressing his lips against mine before turning back to my parents.

"You and I both know you were going to use the expansion of the land for your own gain. Allowing only whatever businesses suited your needs to develop, it was never about the expansion of Cupid. Maybe you hired Sadie thinking somehow if she latched onto me I'd open my checkbook for you once Apollo shot you down or maybe you thought Sadie working here would get her dad to reconsider. Either way it's never going to happen," Nolan taunts, stepping closer forcing my father back. "If you continue to treat her as less than, not only will I punch you in the face, but I will run you out of office. Good luck holding any government position when I'm through with you."

I think my mother, ever the woman for theatrics, is really about to faint. My dad's face contorts, like he actually might fight back or say something but then thinks twice. Whether it's because he's scared of Nolan or because of where we are, I don't know. Maybe he simply thinks I'm not worth the fight but I really don't care. Because finally I have someone in my corner.

"Do I make myself clear?" Nolan demands.

People begin to slow down and notice the stand off happening in the middle of the dance floor, and if there's one thing my father hates, it's negative attention. He nods and my parents walk off without a second glance at me.

The sting from the knife in my back faded a long time ago, my parents turning their backs on me now makes me feel nothing. Nothing but a sweet breath of relief of deciding I'm done pretending I want to be a part of their lives.

There's someone else's life I'd rather be a part of.

CHAPTER TWENTY

NOLAN FOLLOWS WITHOUT A word as I grab his hand and we disappear through the doors and down the first hallway I find.

"Harper, where are we—" I cut him off with a kiss.

Too many thoughts race through my head and I need to spill them all.

Dragging my lips from his, I step back. "You love me," I laugh between the words. When he answers yes, my laughter becomes uncontrollable. I pitch forward nearing hysterics, clutching my chest as my breath sticks in my throat and tears blur his frame. Nolan simply looks at me with a soft smile and waits for me to come to my senses.

It doesn't take long. But in that short timeframe I realize that Nolan looks at me the way I looked at the paintings in the gallery I worked at. He studies me with a delicate eye, rooted to the ground in awe. He looks at me like there's nowhere else he'd rather be, and the realization hits me.

"I don't want to stay here," I blurt out, reaching for his hands.

"We can go back to my place."

"No, I mean in Cupid. I don't want to stay in Cupid, I hate it here. My family is everywhere and I don't want to be anywhere they are."

"Where should we go?"

"I—wait, we?"

"Yes, we."

I shake my head, trying to get the idea that he would so easily leave everything behind to follow me to settle. "What about you? Your life is here now."

"My life is wherever you are. If you want to leave, I'll follow. We can go to the city, visit new galleries every week, or we can find another small town and live our lives out in the countryside. We can go anywhere you want because I'm going to be wherever you are, Harper."

"Because you love me," I state. Not a question, I just want to hear it again. See what it feels like on my tongue.

"Because I love you." He takes my face in between his hands, resting his forehead against mine. "I love you," he repeats, kissing the tip of my nose. "I love you." A kiss to my right cheek. "I love you." A kiss to my left check.

He pulls back but I beat him to it. "And I love you." I confess, pressing my lips against Nolan's. A man who's quickly become my home. A man who's given me everything, when all I ever wanted was to be wanted.

Nolan is the type of man you read about in books, the type of leading man you watch on the big screen and fantasize about finding, even though you know he probably doesn't exist in real life. He was the man starring in my daydreams while at my desk and he's standing in front of me telling me I can have everything I want in life.

Everything was worth it. Midnights, the masks, every turn my life took. Every rejection, every time I was looked over and not chosen. It was all worth it in the end because it led me to this moment.

It led me here.

It led me to Nolan.

"I was hoping it would be you," I whisper against his lips. He blinks as I smile against him. "At Midnights, when a tall, masked man approached me and asked me to go back to his room. In my head, I wanted it to be you."

When Nolan's soft chuckle reverberates against my lips, I see it. The life we live together; learning how to love each other throughout the years, where I'm bathed in the softness I was cruelly denied growing up. I taste the aching sweetness of the life he'll bring me on his lips and in his breath as he whispers back, "I was hoping it would be you, too."

Acknowledgements

Normally I have so much to say at the end of a book, but this story came so fast and organically that none of my usual hesitation hovered around while writing, making this the easiest story I've ever written. This book came together in record time, and I could not have done it without the help of some of the most incredible people.

Britt and Daisy, for being the beta readers of my dreams. You each went above what I ever could have expected with your feedback, and I am so very grateful.

Ellie, who didn't bat an eye when I messaged her about this book at the last minute and for keeping my commas in check.

And Lily, it'll be a sad, sad day if you ever decide to stop proofreading for me. So please don't.

Also by Brittney Lauren

Anything For You
Everything You Are
Whatever You Need

About the Author

Brittney is a Northern California native who spends her nights crafting love stories. When she's not writing you can find her amongst friends deciding what game to play next, performing sing-alongs to her unsuspecting husband, and binge watching period romance movies.

Follow Brittney on Instagram & TikTok:
@brittneylaurenwrites

To stay up to date with upcoming releases, join her newsletter:
https://substack.com/@brittneylauren